# A Bookie's Odds

by

Ursula Renée

**A Bookie's Odds**

Cover Art by *Rae Monet, Inc. Design*

The Wild Rose Press, Inc.
PO Box 708
Adams Basin, NY 14410-0708
Visit us at www.thewildrosepress.com

Publishing History
First Vintage Rose Edition, 2015
Print ISBN 978-1-5092-0318-5
Digital ISBN 978-1-5092-0319-2


Published in the United States of America

**"You're beginning to sound like your father."**

"No, Daddy calls you a thug. I called you a skirt chaser."

Nicholas released her hand and slapped his own over his heart. "You hurt me."

Georgia sucked her teeth. "Be serious."

"I am." He took her hand back into his, ignoring the curious glances from the patrons who had joined them on the dance floor. "How could you say such harsh things?"

"Because it's true. You'll chase after anything in a skirt."

"I do not."

"Oh, forgive me. I forgot your two prerequisites."

"Which are?"

"Big boobs."

"That's not true." He glanced at the mounds peeping from the top of her dress. "I enjoy all breasts."

The room suddenly grew warm. "Stop that." She lowered her eyes, trying to maintain her composure. "People will get the wrong idea."

"What idea? That you're a beautiful woman men can't help but look at?"

"No, that you're interested in me. We both know that's not possible."

"Why not?"

"I've already told you." She huffed. At times, talking to Nicholas was like talking to a mule. "You're a womanizer." She raised her eyes. His, dancing with amusement, stared down at her. "So do me a favor and stop brushing my cheek, kissing my hand, and calling me *amore*, 'cause I'm not your love."

## Praise for Ursula Renée and *SWEET JAZZ*

"The author tells the story in such detail and depth a reader can't help but picture the characters in motion, the unlikeable characters as well as the likable. The story is one of hope, determination and passion for the love of song, music and finding love when it's least expected. I am sure Randy could have given up, packed up his sax and moved on, but he found something worth staying for and very well something worth standing up for…that speaks volumes. *SWEET JAZZ* is just as the title states. It is a sweet romantic story that like jazz has propulsive rhythms played out in harmonic freedom. If you enjoy the laid back sounds of smooth jazz, this is a melodic story that you would want to add to your reading list."

*~Ginger, Long and Short Reviews (4 Stars)*

## Dedication

*A Bookie's Odds* is dedicated to my co-workers,
who patiently listened to me work through plots,
and my son,
who always cheered me on.

Prologue

*October 1942*

"I don't like you."

The announcement came as no surprise to Marco Santiano. He could count on one hand the number of people who actually liked him. Most smiled in his face but would stab him in the back if he were stupid enough to turn it on them. Even the people gathered in his brownstone today, eating his food and drinking his wine, were only there to suck up to him and stay in his good graces.

At least this adversary had the balls to be honest. Except for his mother, no one had ever told him to his face what they thought of him. That alone earned James Collins his respect.

Marco followed his guest into the den and closed the door. The oak barrier did little to muffle the murmurs of the gossips in the family room.

Ten minutes earlier, partygoers had been scattered throughout the house, celebrating his daughter's sixth birthday. Children raced from room to room with no concern for the fragile sculptures they flew past. Their parents were too busy sticking their noses in other people's business to reprimand their hellions.

Despite the games, the clown, and enough sweets to give the children stomachaches for a week, the birthday girl had not been impressed by the activities. She had sat at the front window, refusing to move, until she saw her best friend climb the stoop.

Never before had he seen two people as excited to see each other. The second the late arrival stepped into the house, his daughter squealed loudly enough to nearly shatter glass. The girls hugged and carried on as if it had been weeks instead of hours since they last saw one another.

The other guests had rushed to the foyer to investigate the commotion. Laughter switched to profanity and smiles turned to frowns. The girls, however, were oblivious to the crowd. Neither cared about the differences others used to determine who they could or could not associate with. Race, religion, and socio-economic status meant nothing to them. They were simply happy to be together.

Impressed by the girls' ability to focus on what really mattered, Marco decided to follow their example. After ensuring the friends were under the watchful eye of his mother, he invited James to join him in the room he retreated to each night to unwind.

"Have a seat." Marco waved a hand toward the two red easy chairs in front of the fireplace. "Would you care for a drink?" he offered as he reached for a bottle of bourbon in the last bookcase along the wall.

"I wanna get everythin' out in the open," James replied. He stood in the middle of the room with his arms crossed over his massive chest. The scowl on his face would intimidate a hoodlum into confessing all his sins.

The man was blunt and to the point, traits Macro respected. He loathed people who wasted his time beating around the bush.

"You're not thrilled with your daughter's choice of friends." He phrased the comment as a statement since the frown on the man's face left no question of his displeasure. "How your daughter's able to look beyond—"

"This has nothin' to do with race."

Marco set the bottle on the shelf, then slowly turned to the other man. His heart broke when children teased his daughter about the strawberry-colored birthmark surrounding her left eye. It infuriated him when adults shunned her for something she had no control over.

James shook his head. "Nor does this have to do with the angel's kiss on your daughter's face."

Marco raised an eyebrow. No one had ever used such a precious term for the birthmark. He'd heard people refer to it as a mark of the devil or an unfortunate deformity. His mother called it a *voglie* and accused him of withholding something from his spouse when she was carrying their child. His wife, to the day she died, had simply refused to acknowledge it.

Despite the kind words, James's features did not soften. Lines creased his forehead, and the nostrils on his broad nose flared. The frown he had been wearing since he stepped into the brownstone deepened. Marco could only assume that the cherub who called the other man daddy got her sweet disposition from her mother.

"If it's not her race or the mark, then what is it?" he asked.

"I don't want my daughter around a gangster."

Marco did not like the word "gangster." The term conjured up images of the men who robbed banks,

3

slapped their women around, and dealt drugs. Unlike Leo Darcy in *Midnight Mary* or Tom Powers in *The Public Enemy*, he helped those the banks snubbed…for a nice profit.

"I prefer to think of myself as a financier."

"I prefer calling a spade a spade…or in your case, a crook a crook."

Marco smiled. The man had guts.

He could not hold James's opinion against him. Not everyone was impressed by his career. When his wife had discovered how he made his money, she threatened to leave. She'd agreed to stay only after he promised never to conduct business in the house.

"If you don't like me, then why are you here?"

"I couldn't hold your career choice against your daughter."

With each passing moment, Marco's respect for the other man increased. Since the girl's father liked honesty, he decided to be truthful, too.

"I hadn't planned on sending an invitation," he confessed. He didn't think the girl would feel comfortable being the only colored child at the party.

"I figured as much. Georgia said the other girls received their invitations two weeks ago. What changed your mind?"

"Celeste was miserable without her friend."

"None of the other children would play with her?"

"I don't think she noticed. She was too busy staring out the window for your girl."

He thought his daughter had understood her friend was not coming when he suggested they could get together separately. But, as soon as the party started, she insisted on waiting by the door for the other girl.

She had not cared about the children who came from money or had the "right" pedigree. She only wanted to play with the girl who had done the one thing no one else had…reached out to her as a friend.

Celeste's long face and sad eyes tore at his heart, and he sent a car for Georgia. He did not like his princess unhappy and suspected the other man felt the same about his daughter.

"Why'd you move north?" Marco asked, despite knowing the answer.

The day after Celeste came home from school rambling about her new best friend, Marco had checked out the other man. He knew everything there was to know about the sanitation worker who tended bar at night to not only support his daughter but save for her college tuition.

James's shoulders slumped. His pain was reflected in his eyes.

"Wife died in childbirth four years ago, 'cause there was no hospital nearby for colored folks. Junior died not long after. I didn't want Georgia growin' up in a town that barely had services for white folks and a helleva lot less for coloreds."

"That's why she's not enrolled in her zoned school?" The other man did not react to the revelation that his daughter was not attending the school assigned to her neighborhood. Encouraged by his lack of response, Marco asked, "It's safe to assume you want the best for your daughter?"

"What are you sayin'?"

"What you hate most about me may be a blessing for your girl."

James raised an eyebrow. Though he continued to

5

frown, Marco knew he had the man's interest.

"Your girl reached out to mine. Because of her kindness, I'm willing to offer her protection. No matter where she goes in this city, she'll be safe."

Marco nodded his head at the window. James stepped forward and peered down at the garden.

Celeste and Georgia sat on the swings, challenging each other to touch the sky. Three other girls stood nearby. Their pouts said they wanted to chase the friends from the playground equipment. Yet none of them were brave enough to cross the older woman who sat on a bench and watched. Her scowl dared anyone to bother the two friends.

James's features softened. He nodded. As Marco had suspected, the man was willing to make a deal with the enemy to ensure his daughter's happiness.

Marco turned back to the bookcase. When he went into business, he'd learned people had a tendency to say what they thought he wanted to hear. There was rarely any truth behind the words that spilled from people's lips.

James's honesty told him he would not have to worry about the man going back on his word. There would be no need for contracts, signatures, witnesses, or lawyers. In their case, a gentleman's agreement would suffice.

Marco held out a glass to his adversary. With a nod of appreciation, James accepted the drink.

Silently, the men lifted their glasses to each other. Then they knocked back the liquor and sealed the deal for their daughters' future.

Chapter 1

*September 1957*

He was short. He was scrawny. And his body odor would offend a dog. Yet with all he did not have going for him, he had the nerve to call someone ugly. As Marco Santiano would say*, che coglioni*...the kid was an idiot.

The punk sneered as if he were staring at a slug on the bottom of his grimy sneaker. His friend stood behind him, neighing and snorting at behavior unacceptable from someone old enough to ride the train alone. In fact, out of the four people standing in front of the diner, the young men were the only ones laughing.

Georgia Mae Collins was not amused by the off-colored comment directed at her friend. And she knew she would find no humor in the consequences of his words.

"You need to leave her alone."

She hoped he would heed her warning and leave while he was capable of doing so on his own. No one messed with Celeste Santiano and walked away. Crawled away, maybe. Dragged away, possibly. Carried away, in a lot of cases. But never walked away.

Squaring his shoulders, the punk slowly turned and faced her. Pockmarks decorated his sallow cheeks and nose. Pus-filled pimples covered his chin. His dried, cracked lips curled back, revealing brownish-yellow teeth. Greasy bangs dangled in front of sunken, bloodshot eyes.

He took a drag off his cigarette, then blew the smoke in her face. Her eyes watered from his rancid breath.

"Ain't no one talkin' to yah, nig—"

"I wouldn't complete that sentence if I were you," Celeste warned.

"Why? Yah friends with the coon?" He pointed to the birthmark that stretched from his first victim's left brow to her cheekbone. "Too ugly for real friends?"

Celeste crossed her arms over her chest. Her blue eyes narrowed behind medium brown strands that danced in front of her face. Before she could repeat her warning, a voice announced, "It's time for you girls to go home."

Georgia cringed. She glanced past their tormentors at the two men who joined the group. What she had been hoping to avoid was about to take place. All hell was going to break loose.

"He called Georgia—"

"I heard what he said." Nicholas Santiano interrupted before Celeste could repeat the vile word. He held up a set of keys in his left hand. "Take my ride, Georgia."

Her gaze dropped from his icy blue eyes to the tick in his square jaw, and then to the lead pipe in his right hand. Her aversion to blood had ruled out a career in medicine. It also inspired her to try to prevent bloodshed, even when young men demonstrated a desire to never eat solid foods again.

"Nick—"

"Now." His tone said he would not listen to reason. The chocolate ice cream she had been enjoying moments earlier lost its appeal, and she dropped her cone in the trash can in front of the diner before stepping around the tormenter.

Though the punk maintained his scowl, he was not standing as tall as he had been a minute ago. Likewise, his friend was no longer laughing; he looked as if he was about to soil his pants. Not that she blamed him. Most men did not fare well against someone who stood six feet tall, weighed a hundred eighty-five pounds, and worked out three times week.

Georgia dragged her feet until she was six inches in front of Nicholas. She reached up for the keys. He wrapped his fingers around hers, pulled her hand to his lips and kissed the back.

"Smile." His tone softened as he pressed the pipe into her free hand. "Everything'll be all right."

Georgia shook her head. She knew it wouldn't. Nicholas may have given her the weapon, but he was still capable of inflicting damage with his bare hands.

Georgia pulled from his grip and followed Celeste to the red convertible parked across the street. She opened the driver's door, then glanced back as Nicholas draped an arm over the punk's shoulders. He steered the tormentor toward the vacant lot next to the diner. Gianni Acardis, his longtime friend, lifted the tail of his shirt. The piece tucked in his pants convinced the other boy to follow.

With a sigh, Georgia shoved the pipe underneath the driver's seat, climbed behind the wheel, and started the car.

"It's a shame some people have to learn the hard

way." Celeste slid into the passenger seat. "He should've listened to me."

Georgia pulled away from the curb. "What do you mean, listen to you? You didn't say anything when that punk came over."

"But I spoke up before he called you out of your name." She bit into her sugar cone. "Now he's gonna be gumming his food."

Georgia stopped at a red light and turned toward her friend. "You should've told him no one messes with Celeste Santiano. Not unless he wants to deal with Nicholas Santiano."

Celeste threw her head back and shrieked. The balding driver in the brown-and-white station wagon in front of them peered into his rearview mirror.

"What's so funny?"

"You are." Celeste rocked back and forth. Tears rolled down her cheeks. "Nicky fighting 'cause of me."

"I wasn't joking. Why else would Nick get into a fight?"

"'Cause that kid insulted you."

Georgia would have convulsed with laughter had she not been behind the wheel. Since getting into an accident was not on her agenda, she faced forward and sucked her teeth.

Yes, she was under the protection of the Santianos. And yes, over the years Nicholas had come to her defense more times than she could count. However, she had no doubts regarding his priorities. Family came first, and the punk was getting his face rearranged because of his insult to Celeste, not her.

Celeste slumped back in her seat. "If he's not fighting 'cause of you, what was all that back there?"

She deepened her voice. "Take my ride, Georgia." She switched back to her softer pitch. "Why didn't he give me the keys?"

"'Cause you can't drive."

"New York City seems to think otherwise." Celeste pulled her license out of the side pocket of her red-checkered dress and waved it in the air.

"You only got that 'cause you cried after your last road test. The instructor felt sorry for you."

"Then what about the kiss?"

"That was all for show."

Georgia refused to take Nicholas's flirting seriously. She did not possess the four B's he looked for in a woman: blonde hair, blue eyes, and big breasts. Though her shirts did not lie flat against her, the tops worn by the women he dated strained against the overabundance of flesh stuffed underneath the material.

Georgia smashed the horn to alert the first driver that the light had changed. The man stuck his arm out the window and gave her a one-finger salute.

After another failed interview that morning with a man who treated her as if she could not add one plus one, and then an afternoon of reviewing books that had been altered, she had little patience for the man. Georgia maneuvered around the other car and hit the gas. He barely had time to yank his arm back before she sped past.

Taking the side streets, she avoided the rush hour traffic that would have turned the thirty-minute drive from Coney Island into an ordeal. When they arrived at the Fort Greene section of Brooklyn, she parked in front of the brownstone next door to the Santianos'.

Georgia followed Celeste through the garden

entrance of the four-story structure. The aroma of *pollo alla cacciatora* welcomed her to her second home. As always, Mr. Santiano's chicken made her mouth water.

"Papa, we're home," Celeste yelled.

"Who's we?"

Georgia strolled into the kitchen. "It's me, Mr. Santiano."

The older man looked up from the stove, where he had been dropping dough into a deep fryer. Strands of gray intermingled with his brown hair, moustache, and goatee. His solid physique, however, had not been affected by time.

"I didn't expect to see you 'til this evening."

"We had a little trouble," Celeste volunteered. She swiped a *zeppole* from a plate on the counter next to the stove. "Nicky sent us home in his car."

In the light drifting through the opened window, Georgia watched the man's warm, brown eyes turn cold. "You had a problem at Joey's?" His tone promised unpleasant consequences if he did not like the answer.

Though he employed musclemen to help with debt collection, when it came to his family and friends, Mr. Santiano did not hesitate to get his hands dirty.

"Some kids insulted Celeste," Georgia replied. "Nick took care of it."

He glanced at Celeste, who was too busy chewing her pastry to elaborate on the events. After a heartbeat, he shook his head. "How did things go otherwise?"

Satisfied the man would not storm out of the house looking for blood, Georgia leaned against the counter. "Everyone's fine—" She focused on the black-and-white pattern on the floor.

"But?" he asked when she did not complete her thought.

Georgia's head snapped up. "How did you know there was a 'but'?"

He pointed at her with the spoon he had been using for the dough. "You were fiddling with your fingers. You only do that when a 'but' is involved." He rapped the back of Celeste's hand with the spoon as she reached for another *zeppole*. "Was it bad?"

Georgia nodded. "The books had been altered," she replied as she folded her hands behind her back.

"You told Joey?"

"Yes."

Georgia recalled the disappointment in the man's eyes when she showed him the changes in the ledgers that confirmed his son had been stealing from him. Despite the betrayal, he maintained his composure as he paid her fee. He then mumbled his excuse before slipping out of the room.

A friend of the family for sixteen years, Georgia had known what was to follow. From an early age, every Santiano was taught no matter what side of the law you chose to live on, you did not screw over family. The punishment for doing so was not pleasant. The bloody pipe in Nicholas's car attested to the severity.

"*Grazie, cara.*" Mr. Santiano picked up a plate and held it toward her. "Take one."

Like Nicholas had done earlier when he offered to buy her an ice cream cone, Marco Santiano was using her penchant for sweets to sooth her. Of course, Georgia was too fond of the fried dough dripping with honey to say no.

"Are you staying for dinner?" he asked as she took a *zeppole*.

"No, I promised Daddy I'd be home before he went to the bar," she replied before she licked a drop of honey from her finger.

"You'll take some food with you." Mr. Santiano placed the plate on the counter. As he reached up to a cabinet next to Georgia, the front door slammed open. The boisterous laughter announcing Nicholas's arrival was tame compared to the racket he used to make when he came home from school.

"Hey, Pops, you in the kitchen?"

"Who else do you think's cooking? It's definitely not one of my lazy children."

Nicholas stepped into the kitchen. Neither he nor Celeste appeared to take offense at Mr. Santiano's comment.

Celeste gasped when Gianni walked into the room. "What happened to your face?"

"The prick took a swing at me." He rubbed his bruised jaw. "He hits like a girl."

Georgia rolled her eyes. Gianni had the dark hair and bluish-gray eyes of a leading man and the build of a middleweight boxer. He also had an attitude that straddled the line between respect and insolence.

The chair scraped against the linoleum as he dragged it from underneath the table.

"Watch the floor," Mr. Santiano scolded.

"Yeah, sure," Gianni mumbled as he slouched in the chair.

Shaking his head, Mr. Santiano turned back to the stove.

Nicholas leaned against the counter.

His lips twisted in a smirk and his eyes danced with mischief. Before she could contemplate the reason for his glee, he leaned in and took a bite from her *zeppole*.

"Get your own." She pulled her hand away, too late to save half her pastry.

"Feed me," he said around the food in the mouth.

"Feed yourself."

"Gotta clean up first." He held out his battered knuckles. "That puke's jaw was as hard as granite."

Aside from his bruised hands, he showed no signs of the fight. Every strand of his brown, wavy hair was in place. His gray pants and blue button-down shirt had no wrinkles, dust, or blood. And, instead of sweat, he smelled of cigarette smoke and the remnants of the aftershave he'd applied that morning.

"No one told you to fight."

"What was I supposed to do? Stand there while some punk calls you out of your name?"

"You could've tried talking, or walked away."

"I did." He caught a dishtowel his father tossed to him. "My fists told him I didn't appreciate his comment, and I walked away when they were finished."

Nicholas was a diehard member of the black-eye, loose-tooth, broken-bone club. He gave no warnings before he let his fists convey his emotions. And, while his methods had always convinced bullies to find someone else to torment, she sometimes wished he'd find a less violent means of expressing himself.

Georgia watched as he dabbed the blood from his tender knuckles. Despite her beliefs, she was a member of the cold compress, antiseptic, bandage league and had never been able to turn her back on him when he was hurt.

With a sigh, she popped the remainder of her *zeppole* in her mouth before grabbing Nicholas's arm and pulling him to the sink. She turned on the faucet and shoved his hands underneath tepid water.

He chuckled. "I knew you cared...ow, fuck..."

\*\*\*\*

The expletive slipped out when Georgia not so gently pressed the dishtowel to a cut. The subsequent sting to the back of his head was not unexpected.

"Watch your language," his father scolded as he passed by to answer the telephone in the hall. "There's a lady present."

Nicholas uttered another expletive under his breath. He pulled a hand from under the faucet, reached up, and rubbed the spot his father had slapped on the back of his head.

"Don't look so smug," he grumbled, glancing at the woman by his side.

The smile Georgia had not bothered hiding grew wider. He flicked water on her. As he expected, she splashed water back at him.

At times Georgia could be as annoying as his sister. Of course, what else could he expect from two women who spent so much time together? From first grade through twelfth, they'd attended the same schools. And, even if they weren't in the same classes, they always met for lunch and hung out together every day after school.

Aside from their tendency to act silly, the women were different as night and day. Celeste had cared less about academics. She fussed over her wardrobe, and her reading list included *Glamour*, *Mademoiselle*, and

16

*Vogue*. While Georgia had traded in her shapeless pinafores for dresses with fitted bodices and full skirts, she preferred textbooks over fashion magazines. She did not spend hours fussing over her hair and face. Instead, she wore her dark brown hair in a ponytail that gave the world an unobstructed view of her flawless cocoa complexion.

"That was Joey," his father announced, returning to the kitchen.

"I already took care of it," Nicholas replied.

Georgia tensed, yet she remained silent. He knew she was not a fan of his method of solving problems, but in this case she would not argue with him. She understood the Santianos' code. His cousin stole from family. There was no talking and no second chances. Only the painful reminder that one did not screw over family.

"Joey told me." His father returned to spooning food into a bowl. "His kid should count his blessings. If I'd handled it, he'd have walked away with two busted hands, not one." He looked at Georgia. "Joey would like you to take care of the books for the diner."

"No," Nicholas said at the same time Georgia asked, "Are you serious?"

His father raised an eyebrow. "No one asked you," he said to his son before addressing Georgia. "Yes, I am."

"Why can't Uncle Joey find another bookkeeper?" Nicholas asked, despite his father's comment. He pulled his hands from under the faucet.

"He trusts Georgia."

"I don't like it."

"Then it's a good thing it's not your decision to

make." She tossed the towel at him and turned off the water.

His father laughed.

Nicholas bit back the retort that would start an argument. With his father on her side, it would be an argument he'd lose. Not that Georgia needed someone to back her up. She was more than capable of holding her own against him. Her earlier work at the diner was a testament to that.

Nicholas had objected when his father first asked her to review the books at the diner that also hosted a gambling den in the basement. Instead of taking his concerns into consideration, she firmly, but sweetly, told him to mind his own damn business.

"Don't pay attention to him," his father said now. "You think about what's best for you."

"How could you condone her working there? You wouldn't recommend Celeste for the job."

"That's 'cause Celeste adds as well as she cooks."

"Papa," Celeste whined.

"I'm sorry, darling, but numbers aren't your thing." The older man placed a kiss on his daughter's forehead before turning to the other woman. "Give this to your father, and tell him I send my best."

"Thank you." Georgia's features softened as she accepted the shopping bag full of food. Her eyes narrowed when she turned back to Nicholas.

With a sigh, he tossed the towel on top of a basket sitting on the floor by the entrance to the kitchen. "I'll give you a ride."

"I'm not sure if I want a ride from you."

"How do you expect to get home?" He took the bag from her. "Walk?"

"I could take the bus."

"And you could stop being a pain in my rear." He placed a hand on the small of her back. "I'll be back in a few," he called over his shoulder.

"Take your time," Gianni said.

"I'll keep him company," Celeste added as she slid into the seat next to his friend.

"Or he can drive himself home," his father suggested.

Before the older man volunteered to show him to the door, Gianni stood and followed the couple out of the house.

Nicholas led Georgia to the passenger side of the convertible and opened the door. Though his father did not conduct business in the house, everyone in the neighborhood knew he would not hesitate to draw blood if his family or property was disturbed. The fear insured no one messed with Nicholas's car when he left it unlocked with the top down.

Gianni continued to the red coupe parked in front of the convertible and drove off. Nicholas was not offended by his friend's abrupt departure. They never believed in saying goodbye only to have to say hello when they met up again.

Georgia slid into the passenger seat while Nicholas placed the bag on the floor in the back. Once she was settled, he closed her door, then jogged around to the driver's side.

They rode in silence, and Nicholas knew Georgia was contemplating his uncle's offer. A week earlier, she had confided in him the trouble she was having in finding a job. Before reviewing her applications, interviewers would point her in the direction of the secretarial pool. And those were the ones who had been able to look beyond her complexion. One potential employer presented her with a mop and told her to empty the trash when she was finished with the floor.

The job at the diner was the opportunity Georgia had been hoping for. Yet Nicholas's protective instincts kept him from supporting her. There were some places she should not frequent, just like there were some men she should not get involved with.

Realizing his objections would start an argument, Nicholas decided to drop the subject for the time being.

"I'm wearing a navy blue suit tonight," he announced.

Georgia turned to him and raised her eyebrows. "Why should I give a hoot about what you wear?"

"Figured you'd want to know so we don't clash."

"And why would we?"

"I'm taking you to the club."

She rolled her eyes so hard he was surprised she did not sprain her eyeballs. "You're full of yourself. You don't even know if I'm going."

Nicholas chuckled.

"What's so funny?"

"You'd never miss Nonna's birthday."

"Then who said I'd let you take me? Maybe I'm going with someone else."

Red flashed before his eyes. Nicholas's laughter abruptly stopped. He clenched his teeth to keep his objections from escaping.

His reaction was ridiculous. Georgia was his sister's best friend. There was no reason he should care whether or not she went with someone else. However, the realization that his behavior was inappropriate did not stop him from insisting, "You're going with me."

"You couldn't find anyone else?"

He had not considered asking anyone else. It would not be the same, attending a family gathering with anyone but her.

Instead of telling her the truth, he grumbled, "Why do you have to make things so difficult?"

"Someone needs to put you in your place. It's presumptuous to expect people to jump at your command."

"Just be ready at seven," he announced as he turned the corner.

"Humph," was her only response.

He drove to the other end of the block and parked in front of a three-story building. Cardboard covered one of the windows to Sugar, the bar her father operated from the space on the ground floor.

"What happened?"

"Someone broke in last week."

"Was anyone hurt?"

She shook her head. "It happened after closing. They were gone by the time Daddy got downstairs."

Nicholas noticed the stubborn glint in her eyes.

"What's wrong?"

Georgia sighed. "When I came downstairs, Daddy was reading something. I asked him about it, but he shoved the paper in his pocket and told me it was nothing."

"Don't you trust your father?"

"I want to know what's going on."

"Stop worrying." He brushed his hand across her cheek. "If it was serious, I'm sure your father would tell you." Despite his statement, he made a mental note to speak to his father. Over the years, the two men had become good friends, and his father watched the other man's back just as he did Georgia's.

Nicholas climbed out of the car, strolled to the passenger side, and opened the door. "Don't forget, I'll be back at seven." He reached into the back and grabbed the shopping bag.

Georgia sucked her teeth. "You're so full of yourself." She climbed out of the car.

"Confidence is a virtue."

"Or a sign of arrogance." Georgia took the bag from him and sauntered toward the stoop.

Though she had not confirmed their date, Nicholas had no doubt she would be ready when he returned. Despite her declaration, his assumption was based on habit, not arrogance.

Since Celeste's sixth birthday, she had not missed a Santiano celebration. Because of her loyalty, she was more than a friend…she was family.

Chapter 2

The door clicked behind Georgia, muffling Nicholas's laughter.

There were times his ego got too big and he needed to be taken down a peg or two. She would have volunteered for the job if it didn't inconvenience others.

She was certain he had already told his father she had an escort to the party. Therefore, she would not ask the older man to change his plans and give her a ride at the last minute.

Georgia retrieved the mail before heading up the steps. The tapping from her shoes against the marble floors echoed through the hall. Thanks to her father, the glow from the overhead fixture lit the stairway.

Though it was the landlord's responsibility to maintain the hallways, her father stepped in and made repairs whenever something was broken. He figured the twenty-five cents it cost to replace the bulb was nothing compared to the cost of visiting her in the hospital if she should trip in the dark.

The aroma of fried chicken and okra greeted her when she reached the second floor. The mouthwatering smell was courtesy of the woman in the rear apartment. Despite having six mouths to feed, she would share the meal with the elderly woman who lived next door to her.

The odor of stale cigarettes seeped from the

apartment across from the Collinses'. Whenever the bachelor opened the door to accept deliveries from the Chinese restaurant down the block, a thick cloud hovered in the air behind him.

Georgia turned the knob to the first apartment to the right of the stairs. As expected, she did not need her keys. Like most people in the neighborhood, they did not lock their door unless no one would be home.

"You're late," her father announced.

She stepped into the one-bedroom apartment they had lived in since arriving in New York when she was three. When she turned ten, well-meaning busybodies had suggested her father move them into a two-bedroom apartment so each of them could have privacy. Her father waved off the suggestion, stating he preferred the pullout in the living room, as it allowed him to see everyone who travelled between the front door and her bedroom.

Georgia never took the joke seriously. Her father never had to worry about young men slipping into the apartment. His size alone kept guys from making advances toward her.

He turned from the window, fumbling with his necktie, his forehead wrinkled. "I told you I don't like you hangin' out with that thug."

Georgia pushed the door closed. Her father had never hidden his dislike for Nicholas. She suspected it had to do with the younger man's choice to forego college and pursue a career as a bookie. Of course, Nicholas's insistence on solving problems with his fists instead of talking things out did not help.

"I wasn't hanging out with him. I was with Celeste this afternoon."

"I didn't see her in the car with you."

"Celeste and I had a little trouble. We ended up back at her home."

"And you couldn't've taken the bus from there?"

"You know Mr. Santiano wouldn't have allowed that." She held up the shopping bag. "He sent food and said hello."

"Tell him thanks for me. By the way, what time is that thug pickin' you up?"

"How'd you know he was picking me up?" Georgia was certain she and Nicholas had not been talking loudly enough for anyone inside the building to hear their conversation.

"Who else would he take to his grandmother's party? One of his huzzies?" He snorted. "His grandmother may be in her seventies, but she's still capable of takin' out trash."

"You shouldn't assume the women Nick dates are easy, just 'cause their skirts are tight and they wear a bit too much makeup."

"That's not what I base my assumptions on."

"What then?"

"He's a skirt chaser and only goes out with women who'll drop their drawers for a meal and a movie." He walked out of the room. "Put the food on the table while I get ready."

Georgia glanced at the picture of the young woman on the wall across from the sofa. It was the first thing her father saw when he woke and the last thing he looked at before closing his eyes to go to sleep.

"How did you put up with him?"

She talked to the portrait whenever she was exasperated with her father. She had no recollection of the other woman. However, talking to the picture made her feel closer to her mother.

"At times he can be impossible." She sighed. "Of course, considering what you two had to deal with, I guess his behavior was the least of your troubles."

Her father never talked about the problems he'd experienced when he became involved with a woman outside his race. However, he gave her the journals her mother had kept from the time she migrated from the Philippines to three days before her death.

It had taken Georgia several weeks to read through all the pages. Some passages, like the one detailing her mother's family disowning her because she married a colored man, were so heart-wrenching Georgia had to put the books aside for a day before she could continue.

Georgia marched down the short hall past the closet where her father hung his clothes. At the end, she opened the door to the bedroom no man had ventured into since she graduated from elementary school. Feeling she was a young lady who needed her privacy, she had asked her father to give her the nightly hug and kiss before she retreated into the room. Though he appeared hurt, he agreed to the new routine, and her bedroom became a man-free zone.

She kicked off her shoes, then pulled the door shut again and stepped into the kitchen, to the left of her room.

"You remember William Baptiste?" Her father called from the bathroom.

"Vaguely." She raised her voice to be heard over the water he was running.

Actually, it was kind of hard for her to forget the first young man her father had mentored. Though she

26

had only been four at the time, she remembered the day William collided into their lives.

On a dare, the boy had snatched an orange from the stand outside the grocery store. Too busy looking back at the store owner yelling at him, he ran into her father.

After boxing William's ears, her father made him return the fruit. He then took the boy under his wing. During the school year, he made sure the youngster attended classes and kept up with his work. He also made sure the boy had productive activities to occupy his free time.

Thanks to her father, William avoided the gangs that destroyed the lives of many young men. He graduated from high school and headed to college, yet he stopped by the bar whenever he came to the city to visit his mother and sisters.

"He was by the other night. Do you know he's a lawyer?"

"Is that so? Ow, mother—"

Georgia bit back the curse that nearly escaped when she bumped her hip on the handle to the brown refrigerator. In their house, profanity did not get one popped upside the head. Instead, she would have to endure an hour-long lecture on more ladylike methods of expressing herself.

She kicked the appliance, then instantly regretted her mini-tantrum as pain shot through her bare toes.

"Are you okay in there?"

"Yes, Daddy." She muttered one more curse under her breath before adding, "I just bumped into the refrigerator…again."

"Don't know why you keep bumpin' into it." Her father strolled into the room. "It wasn't a problem when

27

you were younger."

"I was a lot smaller back then." She placed the bag in one end of the double basin sink and opened the cabinet overhead.

He chuckled. "Yeah, you were a skinny little thing. Looked like a twig with arms and legs."

"Thanks a lot, Daddy."

"You don't look like that anymore." Her father pulled out the chair next to the wall and sat down at the table. "You've grown into a pretty young lady."

She pulled out two chipped, blue-trimmed white plates and the stainless steel cutlery. Though they had better dinnerware stored in the breakfront hutch by the entrance to the kitchen, her father preferred the older plates and cutlery that had been a wedding present.

When he married Georgia's mother, people were still dealing with the aftermath of the stock market crash of 1929. Jobs were scarce and money was tight, so few could afford to purchase dinnerware, much less the food to put on them. However, determined to get the newlyweds a present, his family had taken up a collection amongst the immediate and extended members until they had enough for a gift.

Georgia placed the dinnerware on the table that took up most of the floor space. She added two glasses that had once served as jelly jars, to appease the little girl inside her. Though she had traded her bobby socks for stockings eight years earlier, she could not completely turn her back on everything from her youth.

"I showed William your graduation picture." Her father resumed his previous conversation. "Don't know what impressed him more...the beautiful woman or your degree."

Certain of the direction the conversation was about to take, she did not bother to glance up. She spooned a healthy serving of chicken onto his plate.

"I told William you'd be workin' on the books tomorrow and suggested he stop by."

Georgia raised an eyebrow. Her father was going all out to impress the man. He never allowed her near his books.

"You'll have one of the old ledgers open on the table; make it look like you're workin'."

She fought back the desire to slam the bowl onto the table. She should have known better. Her father had believed education was the key to her future, and when she walked across the stage to receive her diploma, his cheers drowned out all the others. But once she had her degree, they could not agree on how she would use it.

Georgia had dreamed of working in the bar with her father. On the few occasions he had been short of help, he permitted her to pour drinks. She assumed once she obtained her degree, he would let her take on a more active role in the business.

Instead of accepting her help, he acted as if anything pertaining to the bar was too complicated for her to comprehend. At times she expected him to pat her on the head before sending her off to buy a dress, get her hair done, or something equally trivial.

"Daddy—"

"Now hear me out, young lady. William's got a good head on his shoulders. He knows the value of hard work. And since I know that silly stuff means a lot to young women, I've heard other gals commentin' on how good he looks."

She dropped into the chair in front of the stove.

"Not every woman's impressed by looks."

"I'm glad to hear that." He reached across the table and covered her hand with his. "Won't you give him a chance?"

Though it had been phrased as a question, Georgia took her father's comment as the order it was meant to be. She, however, could not resist the urge to toss in a sassy reply.

"Is there a particular dress you want me to wear? My lavender one matches my 'Desperately Seeking a Man' sign."

"Don't be a wiseass, young lady." He pulled his hand back and pointed his fork at her. "You just make sure you're downstairs tomorrow afternoon at four. You hear me?"

"Yes, sir."

With a smug grin, her father dug into his food. Between swallows, he recounted a story of William that she had heard so many times she could repeat it word for word with each inflection and gesture he made during the tale.

Georgia pushed the food around her plate with her fork as she considered Joey Santiano's offer. Though he had not gone into details, she knew Nicholas's objections to her working at the diner stemmed from her relationship to Celeste. He extended the determination that his sister not be around illegal activities to her. However, she did not share his concerns.

There was a separate entrance to the gambling hall so the clientele did not come in contact with the diners. And, since Mr. Santiano had only mentioned the diner's ledgers, she assumed the man would hire someone else to keep the books for the den.

Despite Nicholas's concerns, Georgia could not turn her back on the opportunity. Not when no one else, including her father, was willing to give her the chance to prove herself.

Chapter 3

*Where the hell did she get those curves?*

Nicholas's gaze slowly moved from Georgia's low-cut bodice to her narrow waist and the full skirt that covered her hips. Though her hem stopped three inches below her knees, he could still admire her shapely calves.

A few seconds passed before Nicholas noticed the two-inch-high heel on her right foot tapping the wood floor in the foyer of her apartment. He reversed the direction of his gaze, moving to the manicured fingers on her hips up to the frown on her face.

"What?" he asked as he forced his eyes to meet hers.

"I said, you asked me that already."

"Asked you what?"

Georgia sighed, yet all he could focus on were the thin strips of material that held her bodice in place. They would reduce the number of eyes he had to blacken for ogling her too hard that evening. At the same time, his body would have appreciated a better view of what was underneath.

Nicholas realized he would not score any debonair points. Only his loose pants would help him save face…that and not walking into something because he was too busy staring at her.

"You've asked me if I was ready three times since

I opened the door." Her head tilted slightly to the side, and her brow wrinkled. "Are you all right?"

He was not aware he had asked the question once, much less three times. He needed to pull himself together before she stepped back and slammed the door in his face. In the best scenario, she would call the bar and ask her father to come upstairs to get rid of him. The worst scenario would be if she called the club and asked his father to send someone for him.

He did not have much to lose when it came to Mr. Collins. He knew the other man disliked him. There was not much he could do to lower the man's opinion of him. However, if word got out around his family or friends that he had turned into a blithering fool in the presence of a beautiful woman, he'd never be able to live it down.

"I'm fine." Nicholas took a deep breath and squared his shoulders. "Are you ready?"

"As I told you the first time, yes." She pointed to the silver-wrapped box on the end of the marble-topped console table.

Nicholas stepped into the apartment and grabbed the gift. She glanced in the mirror above the table and straightened her soft curls. After a slight nod, she draped a white shawl over her shoulders and grabbed her handbag.

Her light jasmine scent hit him as she walked past. Following her, he began to second guess his decision to escort her to the party. His father wouldn't have had a problem sending a car for her. Celeste would have ridden along, and the two women would have gossiped and giggled in the back like two schoolgirls.

Nicholas admonished himself. What was he

thinking? Georgia was not like the women he went out with. Her drawers would stay up, her skirts would stay down, and her legs would stay closed until she had a ring on her finger. He therefore needed to pull it together and concentrate on protecting her from lecherous suitors. If he could appreciate what he saw, he was certain others would, too.

While he accepted the only relief he would get would be by his own hands, not all of his male relatives were as honorable. There were a few who would not have a problem trying to bed her simply to know what it was like to be with a colored woman. Others would not care about the color of her skin, only that she had the right equipment to relieve the itch in their pants.

As long as she was with him, she was considered off limits. No one would consider touching another man's woman...at least, not while her man was in the same building.

Nicholas drove to Gracie's, the club named after his mother. It was the only business owned by his father that did not have a game room in the basement or back. He kept all questionable practices away from the club out of respect for the woman it was named after.

His father had hoped Nicholas would eventually take over running the club. He, however, had decided he preferred a career in "finance" and dreamed of one day taking over the other businesses from the older man.

Nicholas pulled up in front of the club. After helping Georgia out of the car, he tossed his keys to the valet, who understood the consequences of not returning the vehicle in the same condition it was given to him. He then escorted her past the line of people waiting to get inside.

By the time they reached the entrance, the door was being held open for them. An older, colored man wearing a black tuxedo greeted them as they stepped into the building.

"Everything looks wonderful, Al." Nicholas shook the man's hand.

"When have you ever seen it look otherwise?"

On his watch? Never. Alton McRae had been with the club since it opened, working his way up from busboy to maître d'. In his hands, Gracie's flourished, turning a nice profit for Nicholas's father.

"I thought so." Alton slapped Nicholas's arm. He then kissed Georgia's cheek. "Go enjoy yourself. And, keep him out of trouble."

Georgia laughed. "You're asking for the impossible."

"Come on." With a hand on her lower back, Nicholas maneuvered Georgia through the clusters of partygoers. They briefly greeted a few acquaintances with promises of longer conversations after they paid their respects to the lady of honor.

At the front of the club, they climbed the steps to the dais to the right of the stage. Sophie Santiano watched the band playing the popular songs, her dark tresses (well maintained with the help of her hairdresser) bobbing gently in time to the music. The cane that usually swung from her hand—but never touched the ground when she walked—leaned against her chair.

"*Mi carina*, I'm glad you could make it." Sophie held up her hands.

Georgia leaned forward and embraced the older

woman. "You know I couldn't miss your birthday, Nonna." Georgia reached back and took the box from Nicholas. "This is for you."

"Is it the shawl I was admiring in the catalog last month?"

"You'll have to open and see."

"Open it, nothing. I already know." Sophie turned to the white-haired woman to her right. "This young lady can look at a design and then crochet it without a pattern. Such talent." She glanced back up at Georgia. "So when are you going to stop hanging around that bum and settle down with a decent man?"

"Nonna, I'm standing right here," Nicholas grumbled. "At least wait until I'm outta earshot before talking about me."

"I don't believe in talking about people behind their backs. I believe in calling you a bum to your face."

"Feisty." Nicholas leaned forward and kissed the woman's cheek. "That's what I like about you."

"Flattery will get you nowhere." She waved her hand toward the dance floor. "Go on and get. I'll speak to you later."

"Nicholas, I want to go to the powder room," Georgia said as they stepped off the dais.

"Why? You look fine."

"I want to make sure." She fussed with a curl. "You did have the top down."

"And you can trust me…" His gaze moved down her body again. "There ain't a strand out of place."

\*\*\*\*

Georgia rolled her eyes.

How would he know if there was a strand out of

place? He had barely been able to keep his eyes above her neck since he arrived at her apartment.

If it had been any other man, she would have closed the door in his face and called her father to make sure the offender left the building. However, she knew Nicholas was teasing her and that she did not have anything to worry about around him. As far as he was concerned, she was nothing more than a friend of his sister.

Georgia strolled to the other side of the room and headed down a corridor. As she placed her hand on the door to the women's room, she heard a familiar giggle. She walked past the room, turned the corner, and froze at the sight of Gianni pressing Celeste against the wall.

As he leaned toward her, Celeste glanced over his shoulder. Her eyes grew wide, and her cheeks reddened. She placed her hands on the man's shoulders, turned her head to the side, and whispered something that did not travel back to Georgia's ears.

Gianni glanced over his shoulder and sneered.

Georgia was certain the less than friendly greeting was not a result of her interrupting them. Over the years, Gianni had let her know with scowls, grimaces, and glares of outright disgust that he never appreciated her presence. She was certain it was only the protection of the Santianos that kept him from vocalizing his feelings.

"What'd you want...?" Gianni mouthed the derogatory word he would not dare utter aloud in the presence of a Santiano. The consequence of speaking his thought would be the relocation of his teeth to the back of his head.

"I was looking for the powder room." She glanced

past the man to her friend. "What's going on?"

"I thought I felt something in my eye." Celeste gently pushed against Gianni's shoulders until he stepped back. "Gio was checking it for me."

Georgia raised her eyebrows. Did her friend seriously think she'd buy that cockamamie excuse?

The gesture was wasted on Celeste. She turned her attention back to Gianni.

"My eye's better. Thanks for the help," she said as she ducked around the man. "I'll come with you." Celeste grabbed Georgia's wrist as she rushed past. Georgia peered over her shoulder at Gianni. He glared back at her as he smoothed his brow with his middle finger. She was tempted to return the gesture. At the last second, she decided not to stoop to his level and allowed Celeste to lead her around the corner to the ladies' room.

Two women, primping in front of the mirror that spanned the length of one wall, ceased cackling when the friends walked into the lounge. Despite the age spots covering her cheeks, the shorter one smirked at Celeste. The crow's feet surrounding her companion's eyes became more prominent as she sneered at Georgia.

Crossing their arms over their chests, the friends stood on either side of the door until the women shoved their cosmetics into their purses and sauntered out of the room.

"It's about time you got here." Celeste stepped in front of the mirror, once the door closed. "I was beginning to think Nicky had kidnapped you."

"From the looks of it, you didn't appear too worried."

Celeste's blush deepened.

"What the hell are you thinking? Your father would've killed you if he'd caught you. Not to mention what he'd do to Gianni," Georgia added, despite the twinge of satisfaction she felt at the thought of the young man's castration.

"It's not what it looked like. I had something in my eye."

"Please." Georgia rolled her eyes. "A two-year-old wouldn't buy that excuse."

Celeste sighed. "Okay, fine." She pulled Georgia to the red-velvet-covered chaise. "Gio and I have been seeing each other for a while."

Georgia dropped onto the seat. "Have you lost your mind? What would your father say?"

Gianni had been friends with Nicholas since elementary school. She therefore realized any objections she had toward the man would fall on deaf ears. However, there was no question about what Mr. Santiano's feeling would be about the relationship.

On countless occasions the man had reiterated his wife's deathbed wish that their daughter marry someone in a legitimate line of work. Though the woman loved her husband, she wanted her daughter to never have to worry about her spouse going to jail or an early grave as a result of his activities.

"I know Papa doesn't think much of Gio, but he doesn't really know him. Gio's smart and kind and…"

"He works with Nick," Georgia reminded her friend. "Your father's not going to let you get involved with him."

Celeste sighed as she sat on the edge of the chaise. "I'm sure once Papa gets to know him, he'll like Gio. I've just got to find a way to get them together."

Georgia shook her head. They would get a man on the moon before Marco Santiano liked Gianni. Celeste was his princess, and only the best would do for her.

Her friend reached out and clasped her hands. "Promise me you won't say anything until I figure out how to get Papa to accept Gio."

The desperation in Celeste's eyes indicated she had fallen hard for the man.

Georgia huffed. As much as she did not want to be a party to the other woman's deception, she nodded her head. "As long as you promise not to do anything stupid."

Celeste squealed and embraced Georgia. "Thank you."

Georgia gave her friend a slight squeeze before pulling back. She wished she could share in her friend's excitement, but a nagging feeling said she would regret her promise.

Celeste jumped to her feet and grabbed Georgia's hand. "Come on, we should get out there before the guys think we got lost."

With a sigh, Georgia pushed up from the chaise. She shuffled behind her friend and out of the lounge. Nicholas stood in the hall with Gianni.

"It's about time," Nicholas said. "What were you doing in there?"

"None of your business," Celeste said, placing her hands on her hips.

"Why can't you be like guys? We do our business and get out."

"It takes time trying to look good for you guys."

Nicholas laughed. "What guys?" He glanced down the hall, then back up. "You mean the long line waiting for you?"

Georgia smacked his arm. "Be nice."

"Should I take off my jacket to fight back the crowd?"

"Nicholas!"

"Okay, okay, okay. I'll stop. No need to get upset." He stopped laughing. "Celeste knows I'm kidding." He placed a hand on Georgia's back and led the way to the dining room.

"It doesn't matter. It's not nice to tease your sister."

"Maybe not, but it's fun."

As they approached a table, the occupants burst into laughter. Two men leaned back in their chairs and howled as the two women with them snickered.

"I've got a better one," the larger of the two men gasped. "What's the difference between dog shit and a spade?"

Georgia barely had time to tense at the offensive joke before Nicholas had stepped to the table and grabbed the front of the man's shirt.

"I'm curious." His tone was low, cold, and promised a world of hurt. "What's the difference?"

The man swallowed hard. His Adam's apple quivered. Beads of sweat broke out on his forehead, despite the breeze from ceiling fans.

"Well?" Nicholas lifted the man from the chair.

"Ugh!" was the only reply the man could make as his collar tightened around his throat. His face turned an unnatural shade of red.

Georgia stepped forward. "Let him go, Nick." She placed a hand on his arm.

"Why? He wanted to tell jokes." He placed his face

inches from the other man's and bellowed, "Let's hear it."

A crack echoed through the venue. Georgia released Nicholas's arm and jumped back..

"Let him go." Nonna Sophie raised the cane from the top of the table.

Nicholas, who had not flinched, shook his head.

"Let him go, or the next surface my cane smacks will be your head."

After a heartbeat, he shoved the man into the chair and stepped back.

"There'll be no fighting tonight." She shook her cane. "Do I make myself clear?"

He glared at his adversary, his hands in fists.

His grandmother slapped the cane on the table. The echo from the second crack was louder as the majority of the patrons silently gawked at them.

"Did you hear me?"

"Yes, ma'am," he said through clenched teeth.

"Good. Now go dance." When he did not move, she waved the cane to the dance floor in front of the stage. "*Carina.*"

Georgia stepped forward and grabbed his arm. "Come on, Nick."

Nicholas took her hand and lifted her palm to his lips. He then intertwined his fingers with hers. The onlookers parted as he led her to the dance floor.

As the band began to play "Sway," Nicholas slipped his free hand around her waist and pulled her close to him. He led them in a small box-step that would have had no effect on her if there had been more than two inches separating them.

Despite the knowledge he had been trying to make

a point, Georgia's heart raced from the kiss. She mentally scolded herself for having such a reaction to a flirt. She had always considered herself too levelheaded to get flustered by a playboy. That silliness was for other girls.

"Don't frown, *amore mio*. It's not becoming."

Nicholas's low voice sent a shiver through her. There was something wrong with her. She figured she was too close to him. She needed to place some distance between them. The only problem…she enjoyed being in his arms.

Nicholas sighed. "Okay, we'll skip the lecture and get right to the part where I say, 'No, I couldn't walk by, and I'm not sorry for my outburst.' "

She glanced up at him and shook her head. "What lecture?"

"The one in which you ask if I couldn't have simply walked by. When I say, 'no,' then you frown harder and tell me violence isn't the answer."

"Well, it isn't."

"That's why we can't be together, *amore*."

"No, we can't be together 'cause you're a skirt chaser."

"You're beginning to sound like your father."

"No, Daddy calls you a thug. I called you a skirt chaser."

Nicholas released her hand and slapped his own over his heart. "You hurt me."

Georgia sucked her teeth. "Be serious."

"I am." He took her hand back into his, ignoring the curious glances from the patrons who had joined them on the dance floor. "How could you say such harsh things?"

"Because it's true. You'll chase after anything in a skirt."

"I do not."

"Oh, forgive me. I forgot your two prerequisites."

"Which are?"

"Big boobs."

"That's not true." He glanced at the mounds peeping from the top of her dress. "I enjoy all breasts."

The room suddenly grew warm. "Stop that." She lowered her eyes, trying to maintain her composure. "People will get the wrong idea."

"What idea? That you're a beautiful woman men can't help but look at?"

"No, that you're interested in me. We both know that's not possible."

"Why not?"

"I've already told you." She huffed. At times, talking to Nicholas was like talking to a mule. "You're a womanizer." She raised her eyes. His, dancing with amusement, stared down at her. "So do me a favor and stop brushing my cheek, kissing my hand, and calling me *amore*, 'cause I'm not your love."

****

If any other woman had made the remark, Nicholas would have obliged her and walked away. He had left more than a few women standing on the dance floor, sitting in restaurants, or lying naked in bed because they dared to challenge his commitment to them. They either took him as he was or they got nothing.

However, he could not pull away from Georgia. He enjoyed the touch of her soft hands and the feel of her body close to him.

He inhaled the floral scent she'd dabbed behind her

ears and wondered where else she placed the perfume.

Nicholas's body responded to the direction his thoughts took. He knew he should refocus his imagination or he would spend the rest of the evening in an uncomfortable state. However, he wanted to take in everything about her and commit it to memory.

Though doing so ensured it would be a long evening, he figured he could take matters into his own hands once he was alone. He was sure it would not be as good as the real thing, but he would have to be satisfied with what he could get.

While some believed colored women were easy, willing to give it up at the drop of a dime, he knew Georgia was not like that. She was raised, like his sister, to save herself for marriage. And since marrying him was out of the question, so was everything else.

A tug at his nape pulled his attention back to the woman in front of him and away from his lecherous thoughts.

"Did you pull my hair?"

"I had to do something," Georgia replied. "You had a faraway look in your eyes."

Nicholas was glad that was the only thing she saw in his eyes. "I was thinking."

"What's there to think about? All you need to do is agree with me."

"Agree with what?"

Georgia shook her head. "You'll stop all your touchy-feely nonsense." She huffed again. "You also need to stop using those endearments with me. I'm not one of your bimbos."

Nicholas nodded.

No, she wasn't, and she never would be.

She was Georgia Mae Collins, a good woman who deserved a good man, not a thug like him.

Chapter 4

"That's one fine piece of chocolate."

Georgia agreed with the outburst that followed the low whistle from the woman sitting at the table on the other side of the bar.

Though she did not get home until after four in the morning, Georgia was awakened at eight by her father, who insisted she straighten the apartment for their guest. She knew William was not expected to go past the ground floor, and the unreasonable request put her in a gloomy mood she planned to hold onto for the rest of the day.

In spite of her resolve, a smile slowly spread across Georgia's face when the man walked into the bar. She did not believe looks made a person; yet even she had to admit he was easy on the eyes. He was just under six feet tall and had a lean build. His red polo shirt accentuated the muscles in his chest and arms, and his short, dark wavy hair was slicked back from his oval face.

A young lady sitting at the table near the bar gawked. Her companion did not appear to appreciate the attention she paid to the new patron. The man stood and pulled the woman from her seat. With a firm grip on her arm, he dragged her out of the establishment.

"Billy," her father greeted as he stepped from behind the bar. The men met halfway from the door.

They grasped right hands and slapped each other on the back with their lefts. "I'm glad you could stop by."

"You think I'd pass up an offer to have a beer with your college graduate?"

"In that case, come on over." Her father slapped the other man's back once more as he nodded his head toward the bar, where Georgia sat. "Georgia Mae, put those books away and come over here and say hi to Billy."

Georgia closed the ledger and slid off the barstool. Since the records were over three years old, she had not bothered reviewing them. Instead, she had passed the time watching workers repair the broken window.

Though her father insisted business was fine, she worried. There were a few thugs in the neighborhood who were intending to go into the same business as Marco Santiano. However, unlike the older man, they wanted to offer more than a few loans at higher interest rates. They also wanted to provide protection to business owners…after proving how unsafe things could get without it.

The business had been calm earlier, with a few regulars dropping by to enjoy a quick beer and chat with her father about current events. As the day progressed, more and more customers arrived to have a drink or two before they headed to whatever party they planned to attend. By evening, she expected the bar to be filled with those who wanted to get out of the house and socialize but had no other plans.

Georgia smoothed the front of her dress and patted her hair in place before stepping forward. William gave her the once-over, starting from her one-inch heels and slowly working his way up. He finally reached her eyes, and she saw the appreciation in his.

His gaze reminded her of the glint in Nicholas's eyes when they were dancing the previous evening. Her cheeks burned from the memory.

"I haven't seen you since my graduation party," William said. "You've definitely grown up."

"I hope so. That was…how long ago? Fourteen years? I was only eight."

"Back then, you were a skinny 'ninny." He gave her the once-over again before shaking his head. "Who knew you'd grow up to look like this."

"Why don't you two sit, and I'll get you a drink," her father said, before stepping behind the bar. He had sent his bartender home to eat while business was still calm.

William stepped over to the table vacated by the previous couple and pulled a chair out for her. With a smile, Georgia moved toward the offered chair.

"You used to hang out with a little white girl. She had a mark on her face."

Her smile faded as she glanced over her shoulder. "Her name's Celeste, and she's my best friend." She tensed, ready to order him out of the bar. It didn't matter what he looked like; one word against her friend and he was out of there.

"It's a rarity for people to keep in touch after they grow up. Except for my family and your father, I didn't stay in touch with anyone from the neighborhood after I left for college."

Georgia exhaled the breath she had been holding and sat down. Once she was settled, he took the seat across from her.

"You work in the bar with your pops?"

"She looks after the books." Georgia turned toward her father and raised an eyebrow. He showed no shame from the lie he told. "She's good with numbers."

"I occasionally tend bar." She figured she needed to toss in the truth before a bolt of lightning struck the building and flames consumed everyone inside.

"Now that you've graduated from college, I bet you're ready to settle down," William commented.

"Not yet. I figured I'd work a little. I mean, what's the use of getting a degree if I'm not going to use it."

"I'm sure she'll go out, now that she doesn't have to worry about studying," her father added. "When she was in school, her nose was always in a book."

It wasn't like she had much choice. Afraid she would abandon her studies and settle for someone who did not have a promising future, her father scared off anyone who showed the slightest interest in her when she was in high school. In college, she was so busy with her studies she barely had time to hang out with Celeste, much less nurture a relationship with the opposite sex.

William chuckled. "I was the complete opposite when I was in school. Your father practically had to glue my pants to a chair to get me to study. By the time I graduated from high school, I was so sick of school I enrolled in the service."

"But Daddy told me you were a lawyer."

"While I was in the service, I heard quite a few stories about men discriminated against for being the wrong color. My desire to change things was stronger than my distaste for studying. When I was discharged, I went on to study law. I passed the bar two years ago."

"See, I told you he'd a good head on his

shoulders." Her father approached the table and winked at her.

Georgia shook her head. The man had no shame. She wouldn't be surprised if he already had the church reserved and the preacher on call for the wedding.

She glanced at the bottles he set in front of her. "Cola?"

"No man likes a tight skirt."

"One drink won't make me a lush." She pushed the bottle away from her.

"You'll live." Her father pushed the bottle back toward her and held up a bottle of beer. "To young people going places."

William held up his bottle and tapped her father's. Both men glanced at Georgia. After a second, she picked up her cola bottle and joined in the toast. As they drank their respective beverages, the telephone behind the bar rang.

Her father excused himself. She watched as he greeted the caller. His smile faded to a scowl. With a sigh, he held out the handset. "Georgia, it's Nicholas."

Her brow wrinkled in confusion. Nicholas never called her. Since she and Celeste usually did not go more than two days without seeing each other, he simply waited until she dropped by the brownstone to talk to her.

William stood with her and waited until she reached the bar before he sat back down.

"Don't forget you have company," her father mumbled.

"Yes, Daddy." Georgia took the handset. She waited into he returned to the table before she put the phone to her ear.

"Hey, Nick, what's up?"

"Is Celeste with you?"

"No, we left her at the club last night, remember? She said she was getting a ride back with your father."

Nicholas muttered an expletive.

"What's going on?"

"Pops called here looking for her. She told him we were giving her a ride."

"She's not at home?" Georgia realized it was a stupid question. Obviously, her friend wasn't home if they were calling around to look for her. However, the knowledge of how ludicrous she sounded did not stop her from asking, "Where the hell is she?"

"I don't know." Nicholas's voice cracked.

Georgia gripped the side of the bar. She had to keep it together and think. It was possible, in the excitement of the evening, everyone got the messages crossed. It was unlike Celeste to lie and be deceptive. She was usually reliable, except when it came to…

Before she could catch herself, she let out an expletive. Her father's head snapped in her direction. With a sigh, she turned her back on his disapproving glare.

"What is it?" Nicholas asked.

"I caught Gianni and Celeste together last night."

"Caught them doing what?"

"Getting ready to be friendly with each other. They stopped when they saw me."

"Are you sure?"

"I know what it looks like when a couple's about to kiss." Though she had promised she would not say anything, Georgia felt justified in breaking her word. Celeste had obviously broken hers and done something

52

stupid. "Celeste told me they'd been seeing each other for a while."

"I'm calling Gianni."

He abruptly disconnected the call. Georgia dropped the handset on the cradle. She knew he would call her back when he got news.

"What's goin' on, girl?"

Georgia turned back to the men. "Celeste is missing."

"What do you mean, she's missin'?"

"She's run away."

Dread filled her as she thought about the couple. Gianni was not the man for Celeste. The woman was kind and caring, while there was ugliness inside the man. He was sneaky and conniving and would end up breaking her friend's heart.

Georgia jumped as the phone rang. She snatched up the handset and yelled, "Well?"

"I let the phone ring twenty fucking times."

"I can't believe this."

"Why didn't you say anything?"

"'Cause I promised her I wouldn't tell." Her voice grew louder in response to his. She realized Nicholas was upset, but to blame her... "How the hell was I supposed to know she'd run off with him?"

"I gotta call Pops." Nicholas sighed.

"You'll call me if—"

The line went dead.

Georgia knew women did foolish things in the name of love. Earlier that summer, a sixteen-year-old down the street had disappeared for a weekend. She slinked home on Monday after the man she had run off with kicked her out because his wife was due home.

Though Celeste had always dreamt of being swept off her feet, Georgia had thought Celeste would be more sensible. If she had known her friend would lose all common sense, she would have never agreed to keep the secret.

Georgia hung up the phone and returned to the table. Her father stood, his brow furrowed. Celeste had spent as much time at their apartment as Georgia had spent at the Santiano house. He'd watched her grow up, and Georgia suspected he cared for the other woman as a second daughter.

"We think she's run off with Gianni," she announced as she sat in the chair William held out for her.

"You mean that hood who hangs with Nicholas?"

"Yes, sir. I found out last night they were seeing each other."

"Celeste knew her father didn't want her marryin' a thug." Both men sat down. "This is gonna hurt him." He shook a finger at her. "Don't even think about followin' in her footsteps."

Georgia rolled her eyes.

"I'm serious, young lady."

"Daddy, I don't have any plans on marrying anyone anytime soon."

"Then that means you'll be free to have lunch with me tomorrow," William said.

It was a bold move, yet one that should be commended. As a colored, William was not going to get ahead if he was meek. When he saw what he wanted, he needed to go after it.

"She'd love to." Her father's chest poked out. He beamed as if she had landed a prince.

"Daddy, I can answer for myself."

"Then what are you waiting for?"

"Give me a chance to open my mouth."

"Hurry up. He doesn't have all day."

Sometimes the man made it hard for her to remember he was her father. She bit her tongue as she mentally counted to ten.

While she forced back her retort, Georgia considered the younger man. He was well-spoken and seemed like he'd be a good conversationalist. Though she was not in the market for a man, she figured there was no harm in one date.

"Thank you, William. I'll have lunch with you."

"Good. I'll pick you up at ten thirty?" Before she could ask why so early, William stood. "I hate to drink and run, but I've a few errands to run for my mother." He reached for his back pocket.

Her father rose from his seat. "No, this one's on the house."

"Thank you, sir." William shook hands with the older man, then inclined his head toward Georgia. "I'll see you tomorrow."

Georgia watched him stroll out of the bar. She had to admit he looked just as good going as he did coming. She continued to stare until her father cleared his throat.

"Aren't you glad I insisted you come down here today?" he asked. "I expect it won't be long before women are lining up outside his door. You doin' right by gettin' you hooks into him now."

She pulled her eyes off the other man's rear. "Daddy, please. It's just one meal." She stood up. "Don't start making plans."

Agreeing to one date did not mean she was ready

to rent a limo to take her to the church. She had dreams to fulfill, and none of them included marriage.

**\*\*\*\***

To say his father had been upset was an understatement. The man had gone from worried to livid within fifteen seconds of hearing the news. He spent the next five minutes, before he abruptly ended the call, vowing severe pain when he got his hands on Gianni.

The man was out for blood. Not that Nicholas blamed him. If anyone should have known better it would have been Gianni.

As with Celeste and Georgia, the two men had met in school. However, unlike the women, they had not gotten along at first. They had been rivals, each trying to best the other on the playground. But when an older boy who bullied the younger children turned his attention to Gianni, the boys learned they were stronger as friends than foes.

From the day the two first graders sent the fourth grader running back to his classroom in tears, the boys had been practically inseparable. They spent much of their school years plotting and executing one harebrained scheme after another. And, because of their loyalty, if one was caught he did not rat out the other. Even when Gianni had been caught behind the wheel of his father's wrecked car, the twelve-year-old had not told anyone it had been Nicholas's idea to go for a joyride.

Of course, their parents knew better. Unless one boy was home, in bed with a fever, when mischief occurred, it was assumed both were involved. Therefore, Nicholas had also been punished for the car incident.

"Damn," Nicholas mumbled as he reached for the handset.

He had been unfair to Georgia. Considering his loyalty to his friend, why should he expect the women to be different? Instead of yelling at her, he should admire her for not gossiping. Besides, when the situation called for it, she revealed what she had seen.

"Sugar." James Collins answered on the third ring.

"It's Nicholas. May I please speak with Georgia?"

"Have you found your sister?"

"Not yet, sir."

"Georgia's up in the apartment."

"Thanks, sir. I'll call her there."

Nicholas disconnected the call and dialed the number for the apartment. The phone rang twice before she answered.

"Hey," he replied to her greeting.

"Have you heard anything?"

"Not yet."

"So you're calling to yell at me some more?"

His shoulders slumped. Yeah, he had been a jerk. "No, I wanted to apologize. I shouldn't have yelled at you."

"You think?"

He shook his head. "You're not going to make this easy on me."

"Why should I?"

"'Cause it'll be a bit awkward at lunch tomorrow if you're not talking to me."

"You're so full of yourself." She snickered. The sound was reassuring. She wasn't too upset at him.

"I'll be by at noon. How about we go to Miss

Yvonne's?"

She had never turned down an opportunity to visit the restaurant that served Caribbean cuisine.

"I'd love to, but I won't be here."

Nicholas's head jerked back. "Why not?"

"I have a prior commitment."

He heard the amusement in her tone. Of course the brat did not have a prior commitment. The only person she hung out with was Celeste.

"Fine, Celeste can come along."

"I told you, I don't know where she is."

He straightened. "Then who are you going out with?"

"An acquaintance of Daddy's."

Before they could discuss who she was going out with, where they were going, when they expected to return, what they were planning to do and, most importantly, why it was any of his damn business, Mr. Collins bellowed in the background.

"Nicholas, I have to go," Georgia said. "You'll call if you hear anything from Celeste?"

"Yeah, sure." He barely got out the words before he heard the other handset drop onto the cradle.

He pulled the handset from his ear and stared at it. There were a few things in life he had always been able to count on. Gianni and he would have each other's back. Celeste and Georgia would be friends. And Georgia would be free to hang with him.

In less than twenty-four hours, everything seemed to have changed. Though he knew change was inevitable, he did not like it.

Chapter 5

Georgia was hungry, bored, and her derriere hurt from sitting for two hours on the wooden seat. Despite her misery, she forced the corners of her lips to remain up when she grasped Sister Baptiste's hand.

The older woman beamed as she vigorously shook hands with her son's guest. The glint in her eyes said she was working on the guest list for the wedding that would precede the reception Georgia's father was planning.

Georgia glanced at William. Engrossed in his own conversation with a deacon, he offered her no help. Not that she expected any. He had not come to her rescue when she faced the church mothers before service.

William and Georgia had barely settled in the pew before the older women occupying the seats around them oohed and aahed over the nice girl with the lawyer. They then proceeded to launch one question after another at her.

Who were her kin? What church did she belong to? Did she drink? Did she smoke? Could she keep her skirts down and her legs closed?

As personal as some of the questions got, they did not bother her as much as the women's analysis of her appearance. They were able to forgive her dark complexion because she had the good hair and straight nose she could pass on to her children. These comments were made as they fingered the hair that hung loose over her shoulders.

The organist cueing the choir ended the interrogations. However, the moment the service was over, William's mother rushed over to Georgia, ready to continue the cross-examination.

As Georgia braced herself for the next round of twenty questions times five, the pastor's wife motioned to Sister Baptiste from the front of the church. After flashing an apologetic frown, the woman released Georgia's hand and hurried off.

"That was a fine service, Pastor Peters." William shook hands with the salt-and-pepper-haired man who joined the group.

"It was too long and too loud," Georgia muttered under her breath as she waited for her date to step aside.

"Sorry?" He turned to her.

"I asked if you were ready." She figured that was not entirely a lie. She had asked him the question before the organ had finished vibrating from the recessional.

"In a minute."

He turned his back to her to address the man in the black pulpit robe. Though he was friendly, especially to the women in the neighborhood, Pastor Peters was also longwinded. Georgia realized, once the conversation started, they would be there for another twenty minutes.

With no more women vying to ask her personal questions, Georgia no longer felt the need to mind her manners. She was getting out of the row if she had to hike up her skirt and climb over the pew.

"Excuse me." She made certain her tone indicated her intentions.

Instead of testing her determination to gain her

freedom, William stepped aside. Georgia slipped by him and marched up the aisle and out of the church.

Despite the increasing clouds, the temperature was pleasingly warm. She considered going for a walk, though first she needed to get something to eat.

Since Nicholas had mentioned Miss Yvonne's the previous afternoon, she had the taste for callaloo and saltfish. The dish was usually served for breakfast, but the restaurant prepared it until three on Sundays, for people who attended morning service.

"You embarrassed me back there."

Georgia glanced up at the man who had managed to extract himself from his important conversations to join her. In his blue suit, white shirt, and blue-and-red-striped tie, he reminded her of the community leaders who went to Washington, D.C. to fight for their rights. When he talked to the men in the church, she had heard the strength in his voice.

She was certain her father had seen and heard what she had. It was the main reason he'd insisted she go out with William. The younger man was going places, and when he did, he was going to need a good woman by his side. However, Georgia did not think she was cut out to be that woman. For one thing, she enjoyed eating.

"Do you know who those men are?" He barely took a breath before answering his own question. "Deacon Brown and Pastor Peters."

"I'm well aware of who they are. Deacon Brown frequently visits the bar, and Pastor Peters was hitting on me the other day at the grocery."

"Then I'm sure you realize how vital they can be to my future," William said, ignoring her snide remarks.

"I'm sure getting ahead is important to you, but I was expecting lunch, not church, and definitely not the interrogations I was put through this morning."

"What are you talking about?"

Georgia stared at him in disbelief. Did the man not hear the questions she had been asked before the service?

"William, the mothers put me through the third degree. And they examined me like I was up for auction. I'm surprised they didn't make me open my mouth so they could check my teeth."

"You're exaggerating."

"Like hell I am."

The mild expletive caught the attention of the older women who had interrogated her before service and a group of girls playing hand games. The women stopped chatting and frowned. The girls froze in mid-play, their mouths dropping open.

Georgia sighed. In the heat of the moment, she had committed a triple play of sins—a female cursing, in front of her elders, on a Sunday. As far as some were concerned, her soul was already burning in hell.

"Excuse us," she mumbled as she grasped William's elbow. She led him around the corner out of earshot. "When you asked me out to lunch, I had no idea we were doing this…" She waved her hand at the church. "A warning would've been appreciated."

"I was eager to show you off."

"So, that's all I am? A prop?"

"Woman, don't go twisting my words around." He took her hand and placed it in the crook of his arm. "What do you say we get lunch?"

Though she did not appreciate his brushing aside

her concern, she was hungry. She decided to readdress the issue after they ate.

"I kind of had a craving for callaloo and saltfish," she said as he led her in the direction opposite from Miss Yvonne's.

"We can get that next time. I figured today calls for a steak."

"Next time? We haven't finished with this date yet."

"I like to think positive."

Georgia needed to see how the rest of the date went before commenting on the likelihood of them going out again. Though she wasn't on the worst date she'd ever had, she wasn't having a ball.

****

Whenever he got into trouble as a child, Nicholas was told his sole purpose in life was to aggravate his father. Nicholas disagreed. He had a long list of people he enjoyed aggravating, including the man standing behind the bar.

As he approached the front door, Nicholas had heard Mr. Collins's laughter through the open window. Yet the moment he stepped into Sugar, the jolly noise ceased. The older man's smile transformed into a frown and his spine straightened from a relaxed slouch to a rigid posture.

Nicholas was unsure why the other man disliked him; he was certain it had nothing to do with his family. Mr. Collins doted on Celeste, and over the years he had warmed up to the patriarch of the Santiano family. He even accepted a loan from Nicholas's father to buy the bar when the previous owner was ready to retire.

Instead of losing sleep over the situation, Nicholas

decided to enjoy it. The harder the other man scowled, the wider Nicholas's grin grew. He did not have to break a sweat to get under Mr. Collins's skin. All he had to do was walk into the room and the man's blood pressure rose.

The two men sitting at the far end of the bar turned to see who was responsible for the change in Mr. Collins. Nicholas waved as he walked toward the opposite end. He pulled his wallet from his back pocket and dropped two singles on the bar.

"You found Celeste?" the older man asked as he grabbed a bottle of whiskey and a shot glass.

"Not yet."

"How's your father holdin' up?"

"As well as could be expected."

"So, what are you doin' here? You should be with your family. Or, better yet, out lookin' for that hood you call a friend." Despite his declaration, Mr. Collins placed the glass next to the bills and poured the drink.

"We've checked everywhere," he said before knocking back the drink.

As for his family, his father had Nonna. The woman could offer him the support he needed. What could Nicholas do? Stare at him?

He preferred staring at Georgia. Of course, he didn't plan to disclose that information to the woman's father. It was one thing to get kicks from aggravating someone; it was another thing to get kicked for aggravating him.

"Georgia's not here." The older man smirked. "She's on a date."

"With a man?"

"What do you think? She's out with a dog?"

When Georgia mentioned she was going out, she had not indicated it was with someone of the opposite sex.

"Who's she wit'?"

"A young man who grew up in the neighborhood. He's a lawyer who's going places."

Nicholas wanted to say, "Good for her," but he could not utter the lie. Though he should be happy for her, he wasn't. He recognized the jealousy for what it was, yet he still could not help but hope she had a miserable time.

He placed the glass on the bar as he reached behind him for his wallet.

"Don't bother. I'll run a tab." Mr. Collins poured another shot. "I know you're good for it."

Translation: *I know where to find you if you run out without paying. And if I can't find you, your pops will.*

As Nicholas reached for the glass, he heard Georgia's voice drift through the window. He turned as she stepped into the bar. A tall colored man in a tailored suit walked in behind her.

Nicholas hoped her date had turned out to be a jerk, she'd left him to crawl back into the sewer from which he'd emerged, and the man with her was a stranger she met on her way into the bar.

"If it isn't the happy couple." Mr. Collins's voice filled the room, shattering Nicholas's hopes.

All heads in the room turned toward Georgia and her companion. The older men nodded and waved. Their eyes beamed with the pride of knowing someone who had matured from a mischievous boy to a successful man. The younger men, however, eyed him suspiciously, like he was competition. Not that

Nicholas faulted them.

Every woman, with the exception of Georgia, stared at the man as if they wanted a few minutes in the back room with him. Georgia showed no signs she entertained thoughts of being anything other than friends. But she had always been levelheaded. She did not start looking at china patterns simply because a man glanced in her direction.

"How was the date?"

Georgia rolled her eyes. "Daddy."

With her hand on the other man's arm, she walked toward the bar. As far as Nicholas was concerned, the gesture was too intimate. There should have been at least a distance of one mile between her and her date.

Nicholas was certain Georgia would not appreciate his opinion. He, therefore, kept the comment to himself as he slid off the barstool to his feet.

"Did you hear from Celeste?" she asked.

"Not yet."

Georgia patted Nicholas's hand. It was a simple gesture, but, coming from her, it offered him hope.

"Nicholas, I'd like you to meet William. William, this is Nicholas, a good friend."

"Nice meeting you." Her companion had a deep voice that would command attention.

He was approximately two inches shorter than Nicholas and had a wiry build. However, his suit announced he could afford good threads.

Everything about the man was perfect. He was successful, good-looking, and he had her father's approval. He was the type of man Georgia deserved.

Nicholas hated him.

Georgia squeezed Nicholas's hand again. Though

he recognized the silent chastisement, he could not force himself to do more than give the other man a curt nod.

Before Georgia could verbalize her displeasure at Nicholas's behavior, Mr. Collins cleared his throat.

"Nicholas, didn't you say you had somewhere to go?"

It was only the older man's relationship to Georgia that kept Nicholas from calling the man on his lie. Had he done anything other than finish his drink and leave, she would have gotten upset. And, though she wasn't causing a scene, the nails digging into his palm were enough of a deterrent.

Nicholas slipped his hand from under Georgia's and knocked back his drink. He retrieved his wallet and tossed two singles on top of what had already been on the bar.

"Keep the change."

"I intend to." Mr. Collins swept up the money in his hand.

Nicholas took Georgia's hand and kissed the back. "I'll speak to you later, *amore mio*."

She snatched her hand from his. He knew he overstepped his bounds. The previous times he'd kissed her hand, he had done so to prove she was special to him. This time, however, the gesture was to get under the other man's skin.

With a smirk, Nicholas strolled out of the bar. Georgia was going to have something to say about his behavior. Yet the steam coming from her companion's ears said it would be worth it.

\*\*\*\*

"What was that all about?" her father grumbled.

Despite the shiver the kiss had sent through her, Georgia shook her head. "It was Nick being Nick." She slid onto the barstool he had vacated. "I know not to take him seriously."

"Still, watch yourself around him."

She was certain her father's concern was due to Nicholas's reputation of sleeping around. It was the last thing he needed to worry about. If there was one thing she was certain of, Nicholas had no interest in her.

The skepticism in her father's eyes said he had his doubts.

"Trust me, Daddy. Nick and I are just friends."

"I do trust you. It's him I don't." He waved to the empty stool next to her. "Sit. Have a drink."

"I'll sit for a bit, but I'll pass on the drink." William perched on the barstool. "We're meeting at the church in the morning to discuss the situation going on in Arkansas."

"You mean those colored children bein' turned away from that school?" her father asked. "You goin' down to help 'em?"

"No, we figure they already have people rallying behind them. However, we're sure there are children in other southern states who could use our help."

Georgia nodded. Over the past three years, she had read articles about colored students denied entry into a public school, despite the 1954 ruling by the United States Supreme Court that "separate but equal" had no place in public schools. She assumed the stories she read were not isolated incidents and for every one that made the papers there were plenty others that were overlooked.

The events going on in the south reminded Georgia

of how lucky she was. The public schools in Brooklyn were separated by zones. Therefore, all her father had to do was submit proof of her address.

Georgia did not know whose address he had initially used to enroll her in an elementary school outside her zone area. However, after Celeste and she became friends, as far as the Board of Education was concerned, her primary residence was with the Santianos.

Once she was in school, everything did not go smoothly. Some of the other children and a few teachers looked down at her because of the color of her skin. There were a few incidents of name calling and several physical encounters. Yet always, before anything became serious, Nicholas was by her side, ready to defend her.

Georgia felt a touch on her hand. She glanced over at William, who smiled back at her.

"I enjoyed the afternoon," he said. "We should do it again."

"We'll see," she quickly replied before her father could arrange another date. If it was left up to him, the next outing would have the couple standing in front of Pastor Peters and reciting vows.

"How 'bout I drop by during the week and we talk."

"That'll be fine." This time her father was quicker with a response.

Sighing, Georgia nodded. "Yes, that'll be fine."

William climbed off the barstool. He leaned in and gave her a peck on the cheek. The gesture was as chaste as a brother kissing a sister, and it did nothing for her. Of course, she did not expect anything more passionate, not with her father standing in front of them, monitoring their every move.

After shaking hands with the older man, William waved to the men sitting at the opposite end of the bar.

Before the door had finished closing, her father began humming "Get Me to the Church on Time." Two of the older customers turned in her direction and smirked.

Rolling her eyes, Georgia slid off the barstool. She marched toward the rear of the bar to the door that led to the apartments. She'd had her fill of men for the day…and possibly the rest of her life.

Chapter 6

The beige paint was peeling from the drawers of the steel desk, and rust covered the top of the two-drawer file cabinet. The gray dropleaf stand and green-vinyl-covered chair looked like they had been swiped from a classroom in the school across the street from the diner. The typewriter sitting on the stand was older than she was. And, she was certain, the white milk-glass hurricane lamp on the far right-hand corner of her desk previously sat on one of the end tables in her employer's apartment. Yet Georgia appreciated the trouble the man had gone through to set up an office for her.

"I wasn't sure what you'd need." The eldest son of Sophie Santiano pointed to the adding machine perched on top of a box of receipts in the far left corner of the desk. "Let me know if you don't like something. I'll replace it."

"Everything's fine, Mr. Santiano," Georgia said.

He chuckled. "Every time you call me that, I'm reminded of the little girl who skipped around Marco's garden with Celeste."

"Then what should I call you?"

"How about Joey?"

"That's not professional."

"It's more professional than 'yo, old man.' "

She had to admit calling him by his first name was

certainly more professional and respectful than the greeting his son used.

Joseph's sigh and the pain in his eyes tore at her heart. His towering height and husky build reminded Georgia of an oversized teddy bear. But whoever heard of a sad teddy bear?

"Joey it is," she said.

A smile slowly replaced the man's frown. "Your father's blessed to have a good girl like you. Would you like something to eat before you start?"

"No, I'm fine."

"Then I'll let you get to work." He took a step out the door but paused to say, "Remember, don't hesitate to let me know if you need something."

"I won't."

Once the man turned the corner, Georgia silently clapped her hands and shimmied. The most she had hoped for when she graduated from college was her own desk in a room shared with three other people. But to have her own office?

Granted, her office was located in an alcove in the rear of the diner's storage room, and she did not have a door, but it was still her office.

"Oh, I forgot."

Georgia stopped dancing and spun around. The blush warmed the tip of her ears. What must he think about her silliness?

"I'm going to have a telephone installed in here later this week. For the time being, you can use the one out front, behind the counter, if you need to."

"Thank you."

Though his eyes twinkled with amusement at her antics, he did not admonish her for the unprofessional behavior. Joseph chuckled as he disappeared around the corner again.

Deciding the celebration could wait until later, Georgia slipped her black purse into the desk. Because of the warm temperature, she had not worn a sweater over her short-sleeved, red-and-black-print dress. She wished she could have forgone the stockings, but it would have been too casual, even for the diner.

Georgia sat down, moved the adding machine to the side, and pulled the box to the center of the desk. Numbers had always fascinated her, and math had been her favorite subject in school. By the time she reached high school, she had mastered several areas, including trigonometry and calculus. Therefore, it had come as no surprise to those close to her when she announced her decision to study accounting in college.

Determined to make a good impression on the man who had helped her achieve her dream, Georgia ignored the big hand every time it passed by the twelve on the clock hanging over her desk. She worked through the morning until her neck was stiff from bending over the desk, her derriere was sore from sitting so long, and her morning coffee had settled in her bladder.

Her stomach growled, demanding attention. She tightened the muscles, hoping it would quiet down until she finished typing the numbers on the adding machine. The aroma of callaloo and saltfish did not help.

It took Georgia a minute before she remembered Joey did not serve West Indian cuisine in the diner. Since her imagination was not strong enough to conjure up the smells, there was only one explanation as to why she could practically taste the dish.

Georgia froze. How the hell did he know where she

was? The only person she had told about her decision to work at the diner was Joey. At dinner the previous evening, she'd told her father she would spend the day running errands. And, other than asking her to pick up butter, he had not questioned her.

"You're going to have to look up sometime."

She shook her head. "The only thing I *have* to do is stay black and die."

"Georgia, look at me."

She slowly turned from the adding machine to the man standing over her. Though the corners of his lips were turned down in a frown, his eyes danced with amusement.

"You've got to be the most stubborn person I know. What am I going to do with you?"

"Walk away and pretend you never saw me here?"

Nicholas shook his head, and she saw her future at the diner quickly slipping away. Maybe she could talk him into letting her finish out the day before dragging her back home.

"How'd you know I was here?"

"The moment Pops said Uncle Joey wanted to hire you, I knew you'd take the job. I also knew you weren't going to say anything to your father."

"Are you going to tell him?"

"Of course not." He reached out and brushed his fingers across her cheeks. "Though I don't approve of you working here, I know how much this means to you."

Georgia reached up and grasped his hand. "Thank you."

She should have known Nicholas understood. He had always been supportive of her dreams, going so far as to give her a heads-up whenever he heard of a job opening.

Georgia wondered if William would support her decision to work. Or was he looking for a woman who'd stand by his side, look good, and agree with everything he said?

Nicholas held up the brown bag in his other hand.

"Miss Yvonne's?" she guessed.

"Since you couldn't go with me to get your favorite dish, I brought it to you. I figured we could celebrate your first job."

Georgia glanced up at the clock. It was after one; she had been working for over four hours. Though she had wanted to finish working on the receipts, her body begged her to take a break.

"I need to use the facilities, first."

"Go ahead. I'll get everything ready while you're gone."

Georgia rolled back from the desk. Every joint south of her waist protested when she stood. Ignoring Nicholas's chuckle, she shuffled out of the storage room to the kitchen.

Aware of the concerns about her safety, Joseph had assured her the only way to get to the storage room was through the kitchen. At any given time, either he or his wife would have an eye on the door.

"How's it going?" Joey glanced up from the four hamburgers and two grilled cheese sandwiches on the grill.

"I got a lot done this morning," she replied. "I'm taking a quick break."

He glanced at the clock hanging over the window to the dining room. "You should've taken one before now. I don't want my brother accusing me of overworking you."

"I'll take my break at noon from now on."

"And another one at three?"

"That's not nec—" She abandoned her protest when he cocked an eyebrow. "Yes, sir," she agreed, though she didn't think it would be necessary.

He nodded before turning back to the food.

Georgia stepped through the swinging door into the dining room as the bells over the front door jingled. A couple stepped into the diner and stopped at the booth to the left of the door. They scanned the crowded dining room. Seeing no other seats available, they slid onto the blue, vinyl-covered benches on either side of the enamel table.

She moved from behind the counter and headed into the women's room. By the time she finished using the facilities and returned to her office, Nicholas had set up the food on top of the file cabinet.

Georgia dropped into her chair and grabbed the container with callaloo and saltfish. He had remembered she preferred fried dumplings and plantains with her meal.

"I also got you a root beer." Using the back edge of the file cabinet, he popped the cap off the bottle before passing her the beverage.

He held up his bottle of cola, and they tapped them together. Georgia took a swig. The sugary beverage was just the jolt her system needed. She polished off half the soda before placing the bottle on the cabinet.

"So, is this everything you thought it'd be?"

"Yes, except for…" She reached up and rubbed her neck.

"Let me get that."

Nicholas moved behind her chair. Using his thumbs, he massaged the muscles in her neck. He slowly worked on the knots until she could move her head from side to side without pain.

It was hard to believe the hands capable of leaving a person a bloody mess could also ease her aches. If he was that attentive to the women he was intimate with, it was no wonder there never seemed to be a shortage of those willing to go out with him.

Georgia silently admonished herself for the inappropriate thoughts. Nicholas was a flirt, and she could not fall for his charms. Though she wanted to work, she would eventually marry. She could never see him settling down. All he could offer her was a few moments of pleasure, followed by days of loneliness while she waited for him to tire of his other women.

Nicholas was a friend and only a friend.

\*\*\*\*

Georgia was a friend and only a friend.

Nicholas silently repeated the mantra until it played like a skipping record in his brain. It did not matter how soft her skin felt beneath his fingertips or how excited he got from her soft sighs, nothing could happen between them.

Georgia needed a nice, educated man, one who had a promising future ahead of him. A man who could offer her a peaceful and comfortable life. A man like the one she'd gone out with the previous day.

Memories of the other man extinguished Nicholas's excitement. He suddenly felt a tension in his shoulders and neck. He suspected nothing short of introducing his fist to the other man's face would help.

"Nicholas, your food's getting cold." Georgia reached up and touched his hand. "Sit down and eat."

"How do you feel?"

"Better." She patted his hand. "Now sit."

Her concern over his well-being warmed him. The women he went out with never showed any compassion. It was all about them and what they got out of the time they spent together.

Nicholas sat cattycorner to Georgia and dug into his red beans and rice.

"Why'd you stop by the bar yesterday?"

He swallowed. "I figured your pops and I could hang for a bit."

She stared as him as if he'd lost his mind.

"You don't believe me?"

"I'd sooner believe you joined a monastery."

Nicholas's head fell back as he howled with laughter.

"Seriously, why'd you stop by?"

"To talk," he replied once he caught his breath.

"I told you I was going on a date."

"No, you said you were going out with an acquaintance of your father." He slumped back in his chair, extended his legs in front of him, and folded his hands behind his head. "An acquaintance of your father is the widow who lives across the street from you, not a man who turns the head of every woman in a room."

"Okay, I'm sorry I wasn't clear. But what difference does it make anyway? I still wasn't going to be home."

If he'd known she was on a date, he would not have stopped by and had the displeasure of meeting the other man. Of course, knowing she would not appreciate that answer, he replied, "I wouldn't have interrupted your date."

Georgia leaned over her food and shoved a plantain in her mouth. Nicholas assumed the gesture meant she accepted his answer. If he ever decided to quit his current job, he could consider a career as a BS artist.

"Do you plan to go out with him again?"

She shrugged her shoulders as she continued eating.

"Why not? He seemed like a decent guy."

"You're starting to sound like Daddy. I'll save you the trouble." She held up a finger. "William is easy on the eye." She ticked off another finger. "He's a lawyer." A third finger went up. "The man is going places." She slumped back in her chair and dropped her hands in her lap. "And he's going to need a good woman by his side, so why shouldn't that woman be me."

She had recited the list as if it had been repeated to her more than once. He would not have been surprised if her father had led the cheers. Not that he faulted the man. If he had a daughter, he'd try to steer her toward a successful man who had a bright future ahead of him.

"What's wrong?" Nicholas leaned forward and took her hand. "Talk to me."

"I don't want to live Daddy's dream—"

"You want to live your own."

She slowly nodded her head, her eyes broadcasting her surprise.

"I understand more than you realize."

"Then what can I do?"

Nicholas shrugged his shoulders. He wished he had an answer for her.

Aside from promising his wife that Celeste would

marry a man with a legitimate career, his father had assured her Nicholas would earn an honest living. But, Nicholas was too strong-willed, and the man eventually had to accept that there was nothing he could do to about his son's career choice.

It had been easier for him to defy his father than it would be for her. The expectations were different for women than they were for men. It was unfair for her, as all Georgia was asking was the chance to use her brain. If it were in his power, he'd grant her wish.

Chapter 7

"Admit it. I was right."

Georgia rolled her eyes as she leaned against the black painted railing on the stoop.

Her father shook his finger at her. "I saw that, young lady."

"I hope so. I wasn't trying to hide it," she replied.

"You need to watch yourself. You're gettin' too sassy."

"That's 'cause you're gettin' smug."

"I have a right to be smug." He pointed toward the street, where William played stick ball with the neighborhood boys. "I was right."

Her father leaned back on the stoop, resting his elbows on the step behind him. The position pushed his chest out, not that it needed extra help; his arrogance did a good job of inflating his chest.

Georgia turned back to the street. Her father had predicted William would get along well with children. The younger man proved the older one right when he rolled up his sleeves and organized the game.

For the past week it had been obvious the men were on a mission to prove William was the best catch out there. Her father would crow about a positive trait he was certain the younger man possessed. The next day, William would appear and prove the man correct. Yet, despite his positive qualities, Georgia was not attracted to him.

She had told herself they were still getting to know each other and it was too early for feelings to have developed. But when they were apart she did not look forward to their next meeting.

William whistled and waved the boys to the side as a car turned the corner. With the children out of harm's way, the vehicle cruised past.

Georgia's father stood and folded his arms over his chest. He scowled as Earl Washington stuck a hand out the back passenger window, pointed at her father, and mimicked discharging a gun.

The car continued to the corner, then turned. Once it was out of sight, the boys ran back into the center of the street and resumed their game.

"What was that about?" she asked.

Her father stared at the empty corner. "Nothing for you to worry about," he muttered as he sat back down.

The answer was far from satisfactory for Georgia. Despite her father's attempt to be a role model for the younger man, Earl had decided he preferred the streets over an honest living. Besides working for the local ace, he sold drugs out of his apartment. It was rumored that he ordered a hit on his landlord when the man threatened to evict him.

"Billy told me he wants children." Her father leaned back on the step. "Two boys and two girls."

Georgia wished her father would talk to her about any problems he had. Didn't he understand anything affecting him would also affect her?

His clenched jaw and the glare in his eyes said he either didn't understand or he didn't care. Either way, he was determined to shield her from his problems.

Deciding she did not want to start an argument she would lose, Georgia conceded to the change in the topic.

"What about what his wife wants? She's the one who's going to have to carry them."

"Don't be silly. Every woman wants to have children. That's all you and Celeste used to talk about."

No, that was all Celeste used to ramble on about. Georgia had yet to determine if she was willing to take the chance and felt it was unfair of any man to simply assume a woman wanted to put her body through those changes.

"I've heard childbirth is rough. Why should a man assume the woman will just deal with it? What if she can't?"

"You're not tellin' me somethin' I don't know, girl."

Georgia father's voice was filled with grief. His shoulders slumped, and he stared at the sidewalk. Though it had been twenty years, he still mourned his wife.

"I'm sorry, Daddy." She touched his arm.

After a second, he sighed. "I know you are." He patted her hand. "There are better facilities up here for women. Unlike the south, here she would have the help she needs if there were problems…regardless of her skin color."

"But still…"

"You can't let your mother's death scare you. Celeste's mother survived two births, only to be taken out by a sickness."

She remembered Nicholas telling her about the heartbreak of watching his mother get sicker and sicker from leukemia when he was six years old.

"But you're right," he added. "A man and woman should discuss what they want before they get too involved. Nothin' breeds resentment quicker than one half of the relationship demandin' somethin' from the other with no regards to her wants or needs. In the end, no one, not the husband, wife, or the children, will be happy."

Georgia wished her father had the same philosophy for a parent and child relationship. He never had problems making plans for her life. And, while she did not have a problem with going to college and getting a degree, she did not want to use her education to get a husband.

A horn beeped. Georgia squinted against the setting sun at the familiar red convertible parking on the corner.

"Celeste is home," Nicholas shouted.

"It's about time," Georgia mumbled as she rose.

"You will not run to that boy." Her father grabbed her wrist. "A gentleman would walk over to you."

"Daddy, that only applies to couples." She slipped her arm from his hand. "Nicholas and I are friends, so this doesn't count." She leaned over and pecked her father on the cheek. "I'm sure you'll tell William the news."

Georgia felt no qualms about leaving William, since they had not made any plans for the day. She had returned from the grocery store to find him organizing the stickball game and had only watched because her father insisted.

She sprinted up the street. When she was halfway to the car, Nicholas leaned over and pushed open the passenger door. She slipped into the seat and had barely closed the door before he hit the gas.

"When did she get home?"

"Pops called me a half hour ago and said she was at the house."

"Thanks for stopping to get me."

"I knew you'd want to give Celeste a piece of your mind for all the worry she's caused."

"We'll be there a while. I've a lot to get off my chest."

Nicholas stopped at a red light and drummed his fingers against the steering wheel. Georgia stared at his scruffy cheeks and the dark circles under his eyes. Yes, he teased Celeste, but in the end he loved his sister and worried about her.

The second the light turned to green, Nicholas leaned on his horn and shouted insults to the driver in the car in front of them. Then, instead of waiting for the vehicle to move, he darted into the opposite lane and passed it, swerving back into his lane seconds before an oncoming truck entered the intersection. Both of the unknown but endangered drivers honked their horns at such erratic driving.

"Nick, slow down before you get into an accident. We can't give Celeste what for if we're dead."

He snorted. "I'll haunt her if I have to."

"I'd prefer if I was breathing, not an apparition."

"Whatever." He did not slow down. However, since he did not perform anymore foolish stunts, Georgia remained quiet for the rest of the drive.

Nicholas squealed to a stop in front of the house next to his father's, climbed over the front seat to the back, and hopped out onto the sidewalk. He held the door Georgia had swung open, then shoved it closed before following her to the brownstone.

"We're up here," Mr. Santiano called from the living room.

They raced up the steps to the parlor floor. Celeste sat on the blue sofa next to her partner in crime. A bruise on Gianni's left cheek indicated he had already been introduced to Mr. Santiano's fist.

Nonna Sophie occupied a chair, her hand gripping the top of her cane. Mr. Santiano paced the length of the room. The tick in his jaw indicated it was taking all his strength not to further demonstrate his displeasure at the situation.

"You've got some explaining to do."

"Please don't be mad, Nicky." Celeste jumped to her feet. She blocked her brother from reaching his friend. "We couldn't think of any other way."

Gianni did not flinch or display any sign he was concerned about the outcome of Nicholas reaching him.

"Sit down, Nick," his father said. "It's too late. There's nothing we can do."

Nicholas's face displayed the same confusion she felt. "Whaddaya mean, it's too late?"

"They're married."

Celeste held up her left hand. A band similar to the friendship ring a boy had purchased from Woolworth's for Georgia when they were in the eighth grade decorated her friend's third finger.

Georgia dropped into the chair next to the entryway. Her stomach lurched at the news.

"You're married?" Nicholas asked.

"Of course I am. Gio'd only do right by me."

Nicholas's mouth dropped open. He glanced from

his sister to his friend. A smile slowly took over his face.

"If you wanted to marry, why didn't you say something instead of running off?"

"We were afraid Papa would say no if Gio asked for permission." She moved to Georgia's side. "Aren't you going to say something?"

Georgia wanted to scream, "Have you lost your freakin' mind?" and try to shake some sense into her friend. Instead of giving in to her first instinct, she gently shook her head as she whispered, "I can't believe you're married."

"Neither can I. Everything's happened so fast."

"I don't know what to say."

"How about 'Congratulations'?"

That would have been the first word out of her mouth if there was any cause to celebrate. However, she did not see any good coming from the marriage and could not pretend to share in her friend's joy.

Before they grew old waiting for Georgia to force the word from her mouth, Mr. Santiano stopped pacing. "Ladies, I need to discuss a few things with Gianni," he announced. "Go upstairs and talk."

Celeste took Georgia's hand. "Come on."

Georgia followed her friend out of the room. They ran up the two flights to the top floor, which Celeste and Nicholas had shared until he moved out.

"You still haven't said anything," Celeste said once they were in her bedroom.

"I'm in shock." Georgia plopped down on the white floral quilt covering the full-sized bed. It was as honest as she could get without hurting her friend's feelings.

"I know." Celeste dropped to her knees in front of Georgia. "Things didn't happen as I always said I wanted it. But you have to understand we had to do it this way. Papa would've never agreed."

"Whose idea was it to elope?"

"Gio's."

Georgia had suspected as much. Celeste would never have come up with the idea of going behind her father's back.

"I was so scared, and it took him a lot of convincing. But I finally agreed this was the best way."

"But don't you think this is sudden? I mean, how long have you've been going out?"

"It doesn't matter. We've known each other most of our lives."

"And you didn't want to consider your options?"

"What options? If you haven't noticed, I didn't have any." Celeste pointed to her birthmark. "Not with this damn thing on my face."

"Celeste, there's nothing wrong with you. Someone who's really good at heart won't give too figs about your birthmark."

"And I found that person. Gio wanted me despite this thing." Celeste sighed.

"Still, there are others out there."

"Not for me." Georgia opened her mouth, but Celeste held up her hand to stop her. "It's easy for you to talk about options. You're beautiful, so you have choices."

"What are you talking about?"

"I've seen men, both colored and white, stare at you when you walk into a room. When you're finally ready to get married, you'll have more than enough men to pick from. Me…" Celeste shook her head. "I don't have the luxury of playing games. If Gio slipped away there might not be another. And I'll be damned if I end up unmarried and childless, taking care of my elderly father."

It broke Georgia's heart that Celeste thought so little of herself. She was certain her friend would have found someone decent if she had waited.

"Please don't be upset with me," Celeste said.

"I'm not mad at you." Georgia forced a grin on her face. She did not want Gianni to come between them. "I just want the best for you."

"This is the best." Celeste moved from the floor to the bed. She threw her arms around Georgia. "You'll see, I'm going to be happy."

Though the last thing she felt was joy, Georgia embraced her. She figured the gesture was enough to convey how much she cared.

Georgia stayed to the celebratory dinner…if one could call it a celebration. Nonna Sophie refused to speak to the newlyweds. Mr. Santiano showed no emotion. Even the groom looked like he wanted to be anywhere but there.

The only ones in a celebratory mood were Celeste, who had hooked a husband, and Nicholas, because the husband was his best friend.

Once dinner was over, Georgia insisted she needed to get back home. She hugged everyone, with the exception of Gianni, then followed Nicholas to his car. She settled into the passenger seat and stared at her hands in her lap.

Georgia finally glanced up after she felt the tug on her ponytail. They were parked in front of the bar. She had spent the entire ride silently brooding.

She turned to Nicholas. He cocked an eyebrow.

"Cat's got your tongue?"

"I've a lot on my mind," she replied.

"Nothing should be worrying that pretty little head of yours."

Georgia shook her head.

"Why? You're not happy for Celeste and Gianni?"

"I'm surprised your father agreed to the union."

"Why wouldn't he? Gianni will make a good husband."

"He promised your mother that Celeste would marry someone with a legitimate job."

"I'm sure they'll work something out."

She would have preferred if that included Mr. Santiano telling his son-in-law to go to hell and never return. A swift kick in the rear to help him on his way would also work.

"If you frown any harder, your bottom lip's going to drag on the floor. What's going on?"

Georgia debated over whether or not she should disclose her suspicions. Her best friend's husband was Nicholas's best friend. However, she wondered how much of a friend she was being by keeping her suspicions to herself.

Nicholas poked her ribs.

Georgia giggled. "Stop." She squirmed closer to the door.

He poked her again. "Why should I?"

"'Cause I'm ticklish." She slapped at his hand.

"Then it'd be in my best interest to continue, until I get information."

He moved to poke her again. She should have

known the man would stoop to underhanded techniques to get her to talk.

"Okay, okay, okay," she conceded. "I'll tell you."

"Well?" he asked, after a minute passed.

Georgia took a deep breath. It was now or never. "Gianni's not the right man for Celeste." She rushed through the words. Strangely, saying the words did not relieve the pressure in her chest. It felt like whatever was sitting on her got heavier.

A minute passed before he asked, "Why do you say that?"

Georgia shrugged.

"No, that's not good enough." Nicholas sat back. "You make a statement like that, you better have something to back it up."

She sighed. "It's a feeling I get whenever I'm around him."

"You're saying my friend's not good enough for my sister 'cause of a feeling you have? Please tell me there's more."

"No, but my feelings have never been wrong."

Nicholas's fingers drummed the top of the steering wheel. He only became fidgety when he was pissed.

"Apologize."

Georgia shook her head. Her father had taught her never to apologize for speaking her mind. Of course, he also told her to think before she spoke or else she would have to face the consequences of her words.

"So, is that it?"

"Yes," she replied despite the feeling she was about to learn the consequences of speaking out against his friend.

Nicholas shifted the car into drive and waited.

Knowing what he wanted, Georgia climbed out of the car.

"Nicholas—"

"Close the door."

With a sigh, she obeyed. The door barely clicked before he slammed his foot on the gas. The car squealed around the corner.

Though she knew he was not going to return, Georgia remained on the corner, long after the sound of the squealing tires faded. In one afternoon, she had lost her two best friends, and she felt as if her world had come to an end.

## Chapter 8

The explosion from his knuckles slamming against the wood sent a pain shooting from the base of Nicholas's skull to his forehead. He wanted to curl up in a corner and whimper. However, his desire to make things right with Georgia overrode his need for coddling.

He would have stopped by the previous day to talk with her, but he'd been too busy nursing the hangover from hell. After driving off, he had returned to his father's house and insisted on taking Gianni out for a drink under the guise of celebrating his friend's nuptials. In reality, he wanted to drink until he could no longer feel the disappointment of Georgia's words.

For someone who believed in equality, she had some nerve, looking down on his friend. And then to blame her suspicions on a feeling? He took that as a copout. She did not say what she truly felt: she did not think Gianni was good enough.

After considerable thought, Nicholas realized Georgia had never really had the chance to get to know Gianni. When they were children, the boys spent more time at Gianni's apartment than they did at the Santianos' house. The situation could be remedied if the two couples hung out a few times.

After a minute, Nicholas knocked again. He had barely lowered his hand before the door swung open and he was staring at a less than amused colored man wearing green cotton pajamas.

"What the hell do you want?" Mr. Collins grumbled.

"I'm here to drive Georgia to…" Nicholas barely caught himself before he revealed Georgia's secret.

"Drive her where?"

"We were…we were gonna hang out."

"Someone forgot to mention it to her. She left out of here twenty minutes ago."

Shocked, Nicholas glanced at his watch. He stared at it a minute before he realized the damn thing had stopped.

"What time is it?"

"Time you realize some people work nights and sleep during the day." The man stepped back and slammed the door in Nicholas's face.

The dismissal told Nicholas he had not redeemed himself in the other man's eyes. Not that he cared. Nicholas's only concern was Georgia. After he failed to show up at seven, she had probably assumed he was too mad to stick to the routine of picking her up and driving her to the diner.

Nicholas headed back to his car. If he took the side streets, he could arrive at the diner before her bus, which had to stop to pick up and drop off passengers. He, however, had not considered the school buses that drove down the middle of the narrow streets, making it impossible for him to go around. When he was finally clear of the school bus, he had to deal with crossing guards who refused to let traffic move as long as a child was in sight, even when the youngsters were a half a block away.

By the time he reached the diner, Georgia was waiting at the corner for the light to change. He made a u-turn and double-parked in front of the diner.

Nicholas used to lecture her on daydreaming when she was by herself. Her lack of reaction to his squealing tires said she had not broken the habit.

Oblivious to her surroundings, she strolled into the restaurant. Nicholas did not bother rushing after her. Once she reached her office, there was nowhere else for her to go.

"You're here kinda late today," his uncle commented as Nicholas stepped into the kitchen. "Traffic?"

"Overslept," he replied, deciding he'd rather not go into details about his overindulgence.

"Still nursing your hangover?" His uncle chuckled.

Nicholas slouched against a wall. He didn't need to discuss his less than finest moment. His father had already spread the word about him sleeping it off on his sofa. Those men gossiped more than hags.

"What's so bad you had to find the answer in the bottom of a bottle?"

Though he realized his uncle was only trying to help, Nicholas did not want to discuss the argument between Georgia and himself with anyone other than the woman involved. "I'd rather not talk about it."

The older man transferred two slices of pancetta to a plate. "That's okay. You don't have time anyway."

"Why not?"

"Your father left a message in case you stopped by. He wants you to meet him at Gracie's."

Nicholas preferred talking to Georgia over seeing his father. However, unless he had a good excuse, like he was in the middle of another job his father had assigned to him, he did not ignore a summons. Besides, whatever it was would not take long. He would be back at the diner before Georgia left for the day.

"I'll be back," Nicholas said before he walked out of the kitchen.

The drive back to the northern part of the borough took only a half hour. Nicholas parked behind his father's black town car. The driver's face was obscured behind the newspaper he was reading.

Nicholas followed two men pulling the red carpet inside to be cleaned. He waved to a few workers who had been employed by his father for years.

"He's in the back," Alton called from across the room.

He nodded his gratitude for the information before he headed down the hall. In the office, his father sat behind the desk, several papers scattered in front of him. Gianni slouched on a brown leather sofa at the right. Nicholas turned the back of a matching chair to the wall to see both men.

"I'm glad you were finally able to zip it up long enough to join us," his father mumbled.

"I had to drive up from Coney Island." Nicholas dropped into his seat. "But now that you put the idea in my head, I might just look up someone."

Though he had no intention of doing so, he made the comment to rile the older man. His first priority when they finished was to return to the diner.

"It'll have to wait. We have business to discuss."

Nicholas cocked an eyebrow. The last time he'd met with his father at Gracie's, the older man was still trying to convince him to take over running the club.

"Whaddaya need?"

His father glanced toward the sofa. "I remember what it was like after I married Gracie. We lived in my place for a year before I bought the house. The apartment was barely big enough for one, much less two. I won't have Celeste living in a shithole where you banged your broads. Therefore, I'm buying you a house."

"Appreciate it." Gianni sniffed. There was no emotion in his voice. He continued to slouch on the sofa.

To a stranger, it would appear as if he did not care. Nicholas, however, knew his friend was grateful. Gianni never got excited over anything. He also did not believe in wasting his breath to say something unless he meant it.

"I know someone who's got a place to sell," his father continued. "We'll go over later and look at it." He sifted through the papers on the desk. "Have you thought about how you're going to support my princess?"

Gianni shrugged his shoulders.

"Since you don't have any ideas, I'll help you out. I bought this club for Nick, but he's determined to be a thug. Since he doesn't want it, I'm giving it to you as a wedding present."

Surprise flashed in Gianni's eyes. The expression lasted a second before his face went blank.

"I've got a job."

"As of this moment, you no longer work or hang out with Nick. You're a married man, and you're going to act like one. You've been friends with the family long enough to know their mother didn't want them around hustlers." The older man pointed to Nicholas. "There was nothing I could do about him, but I swore Celeste would marry a decent man who earned an honest living, and I'll be damned if I break my word."

"I don't know nothing about running a club."

"You'll learn."

Gianni sat forward and glared at his father-in-law. Nicholas wondered if his friend was still drunk. There was only so much his father would take before he sprang out of his chair and demonstrated why people feared him.

The tension escalated as his father sat back. His right eyelid twitched. It was the only warning an adversary got before he went for blood.

Nicholas shifted in his seat, prepared to jump between the two men. If they came to blows, no matter who won, he'd lose.

After a second, Gianni averted his gaze. While some would consider him a punk for turning away, Nicholas saw his friend's action as a sign that he came to his senses. Only a person with a death wish challenged a bull with nothing more than his bare hands.

"You'll need to read through those." His father slapped some papers on the corner of the desk. "I also suggest you familiarize yourself with the books." He patted a ledger under his right arm. "I always check behind the bookkeepers. Makes it harder for them to steal from you. But you'll have plenty of time to do all that." His father glanced past Nicholas and waved to the empty chair. "Come, have a seat."

The Santianos' lawyer walked into the office. The family had retained the services of the middle-aged man when he graduated from law school twenty years earlier.

For the next couple of hours various lawyers and accountants stopped by with papers that needed to be read, signed, and witnessed in order to officially transfer the club to Gianni. During the transactions, Gianni slouched in the sofa. He barely glanced at the papers handed to him. He simply signed his name where indicated before passing the papers back to the lawyer.

Nicholas assumed his friend was overwhelmed. It was only natural. A week ago, Gianni was a single man who had only himself to think of. Now he was suddenly thrust into the role of husband and business owner, roles most men had weeks, months, even years to prepare for. Roles both of them had sworn they would never be lassoed into.

****

Georgia's fingers struck the desk where buttons would have been had the adding machine not been snatched away. She turned her head as far as her stiff neck allowed and glanced at the man frowning down at her.

"You broke your word," Joey mumbled. "You promised you'd take lunch at noon. It's after two."

Georgia looked at the clock. Sure enough, she had been pounding away at the machine for five hours.

"I'm sorry."

She slumped back in the chair. Without Nicholas walking in with food, she had lost track of time. Of course, the only one she had to blame for his absence was herself. What else could she have expected after she said Gianni was not good enough for Celeste? That

Nicholas would turn his back on his friend for her?

"What's going on?"

Though she wanted to talk, she realized the outcome could go one of two ways. Joey would take her suspicions about Gianni into consideration, or he could resent her accusations. If the former, what could he do? Celeste and Gianni were already married. However, there was no doubt in her mind what he would do if the latter occurred. She'd be out of a job.

Georgia shook her head. "It's nothing."

"Young people. Why you never want to talk to us old folks? You think we won't understand?"

"No, it's not that. It's just something I need to work out on my own."

He patted her shoulder. "You ever want to talk, you let me know."

She forced a small grin on her face as she nodded.

"Good. Now go get cleaned up for lunch."

Joey waited until Georgia stood and stepped back before returning the adding machine to the desk.

She slowly walked out of the storage room, trying to work the stiffness from her legs. With Nicholas not speaking to her, she would have to find another way to keep time under control. She could not have Joey telling her when it was time for a break. He was too busy preparing the orders for the lunch crowd.

As she took care of her needs, she figured a half hour break was all she would need. She could then work the rest of the afternoon and finish a little after four. If she left then, and traffic was good, she would make it home just after five-thirty, the same time she would have arrived if Nicholas drove her.

Georgia's stomach growled, spurring her to hurry

up in the bathroom. After washing her hands, she stepped back into the dining room. She stopped short and stared at the man behind the counter removing money from the register.

"What are you doing?"

Joey's youngest son peered over his shoulder. Beads of sweat covered his forehead. His lids drooped over glassy eyes. A cast covered his right arm, which Nicholas had broken two weeks earlier.

His lip curled back, and he sneered at her. "Mind your own damn business." His left hand shook as he shoved cash into his pants pocket.

Georgia rushed behind the counter. "I'm not going to let you do this."

"Screw you." He shoved her aside.

Though he was larger than she, Georgia refused to stand by and watch the man steal from her employer. With both hands, she pushed him away from the register.

He stumbled back several steps before he caught himself. The glint in his eyes said nothing was going to stand in the way of his prize. Georgia refused to back down, but her determination was no match against his strength. With his good hand he shoved her against the wall with such force it upset the clock over their heads.

The edge of the timepiece struck the man on the head on its way to the floor. He shook off the blow as if he had been hit with a pillow. Georgia barely heard the crash against the linoleum over the sound of her racing heart.

The dining room was empty, and there was no one to help her as he pressed his cast against her throat. She suddenly realized how desperate the man was. He was willing to hurt her—possibly kill her—to get what he wanted.

She reached toward the small counter beneath the kitchen window for a weapon. Her fingertips brushed against the chrome napkin dispenser, but the smooth surface made it impossible for her to get a grip on it.

The cast pressed harder against her throat. It became harder to breathe. As her focus began to fade, she heard a roar. A second later, the arm was ripped away from her throat.

Georgia closed her eyes and coughed. When she opened her eyes, she was staring at Joey's wide back.

"You got it all wrong," the young man shouted. "I saw her take money from the register. I was trying to stop her."

Joey did not verbally respond to the accusation. He reached into his son's pocket and pulled out the twenties that had been sticking out. He tossed the money behind him.

Georgia heard the sound of a fist smacking a face. It was followed by the thud of a body hitting the floor.

Joey spun around. "Are you okay?"

Her hand rose to her throat.

"Go in the kitchen."

Walking backwards, Georgia stepped out of the main room. She jumped at the sound of a body being slammed against the wall. A blubbering voice stumbled over another excuse. He was interrupted by a bellow.

The rage she heard from her employer sent her scurrying back to her office. Georgia dropped into her chair, braced her elbows on the desk, and covered her face with her hands.

She shook at the thought of what would have

happened if Joey had not come out when he did. For the first time she wondered if she had done the right thing, taking this job. Everyone, including herself, had worried about the patrons who frequented the gaming rooms in the basement level. No one considered what could happen if Joey's son returned. They assumed a beating from Nicholas would be enough to deter him from trying anything else.

Georgia jumped as a hand touched her shoulder. Joey stepped back, his hands up indicating he would not hurt her. His eyes reflected his sadness.

"I'm sorry, Joey."

"There's nothing for you to be sorry for. If anything, I should be apologizing for not looking out for you."

"But you couldn't have known."

"Yes, I did." His shoulders drooped. "He's on drugs. I've known it for years. I've just been denying it."

"But how...*why*..."

It made no sense. Joey was a good man. Except for the gambling hall in the basement of the diner, he was not involved in any illegal activity. His children had a good home, went to nice schools, and got everything they wanted.

He plopped onto her guest chair. "There's no rhyme or reason why some people mess with that junk. None of my others bothered with it, and I gave him the same things I gave them." He pulled a wad of cash out of his pocket and dropped it on the desk.

"What's this?"

"I figured, after that, you'd want your pay so you could get out of here."

Georgia pushed the money back toward him. She could not quit her job. There was no telling if she'd ever get another one. "If you don't mind, I'd like to stay."

Joey watched her for a minute before he took the money. "Wait here." He got up and walked out of the room. Georgia heard movement in the kitchen. He returned in less than a minute, carrying a handgun small enough to fit in her purse.

"Do you know how to use this?"

She nodded as she reached for the piece. Eight years earlier, her cousins had taught her how to handle a weapon, when she visited their farm in the state she had been named after.

"As long as you work here, I want you to carry this."

Georgia knew every other man in her life would disapprove of her possessing a gun. As far as they were concerned, her protection was their concern. However, if she was going to prove she was capable of handling herself in the workplace, she could not expect them to save her at every turn.

**** 

Nicholas glanced at his watch. It was time for him to buy a new one. Though the second hand was moving from one number to the next, it was doing so much too slowly for his tastes.

Once the papers had been signed and the books were reviewed, Nicholas's father insisted on introducing Gianni to the staff. Yet instead of asking everyone to gather in the dining room to hear one general announcement, the older man walked Gianni around to meet with each person. He assured everyone the change in ownership would have no impact on the business.

Once the staff had been informed of the change, the three men had a late lunch at a deli around the corner from the club.

"You've somewhere more important you need to be?" his father asked as they stepped out of the restaurant.

"Yes, I do."

Nicholas glanced up. His father's frown said he did not appreciate the honest answer.

"You young people have no respect." The older man shook his head. "You might as well take off. You're not paying attention to me anyway."

"I'll meet up with you tomorrow," Nicholas told his father, then slapped Gianni on the shoulder. "I'll catch up with you later."

He hurried back to his car. He waved to Alton, who was outside overseeing the preparations for that evening. The red carpet had been vacuumed and laid out, the awning cleared of debris, and the potted flowers on either side of the door had been watered and pruned.

Nothing escaped Alton's attention. He put himself in the customers' shoes, anticipating their likes and dislikes. He offered the former from the moment the patrons approached the venue and corrected the latter before they came to anyone else's attention.

Gianni was taking on a big responsibility. However, with Alton's help, Nicholas was certain his friend would not have a problem learning the ropes.

After an uneventful drive back to the diner, Nicholas strolled into the kitchen. His aunt glanced up

Ursula Renée

from where she was preparing a grilled cheese sandwich. He kissed her on the cheek before swiping a French fry draining in the fryer basket.

The theft earned him a slap on the back of his hand. However, it was not enough to teach him a lesson. He grabbed another French fry before he headed down the hall to the storage room. He stopped short at the alcove, where his uncle sat at the desk, frowning at the two neat stacks of receipts in the center of the desk.

"Where's Georgia?"

"I sent her home."

"What…why?" Nicholas hoped their disagreement had not affected her performance. He was ready to plead for her job if necessary.

The older man opened his mouth, but stopped as if he had to think about his next words. After a few seconds, he shook his head. "She worked too hard."

The explanation was believable. When she was younger, Georgia refused to take breaks until her homework was completed. He was certain she had the same commitment to her job. She would not leave anything undone unless forced to.

However, the man's inability to look him in the eye made Nicholas suspect something more was going on. Certain if he tried to dig for more information his uncle would tell him it was none of his business, he decided he'd get the truth from Georgia.

"When did you send her home?"

"About three."

Nicholas glanced at the clock over the desk. It had only been a half hour. If he hurried, he could get back to her place the same time she did, maybe sooner.

With a quick nod, he hurried out to his car. His

106

prediction, however, had turned out wrong. The dismissal of the school across the street from the diner caused a back-up for fifteen minutes. When he finally managed to get out of the neighborhood, a fender bender and argument between the parties involved caused the next delay. By the time he managed to drive around the accident, he was ready to jump out of the car and knock the rivals' heads together.

His frustration nearly reached its peak when an inexperienced traffic cop caused a traffic jam. It took all his strength to keep his grip on the steering wheel and not bang his head on it instead.

By the time Nicholas caught up with Georgia, she was crossing the street to her apartment. As she placed her foot on the first step to the stoop, someone called her name. She turned back and ran to the man who had taken her out two Sundays back.

They exchanged a few words before he took her hand. With their fingers interlocked, they strolled up the block.

Nicholas watched the happy couple. Despite his disdain for the other man, he could not interrupt them. That was Georgia's future, and he had no right to interfere. Especially since he could never offer her the stability and quiet life she deserved.

With a sigh, Nicholas hit the gas. There'd be another chance for them to talk. And, if not, it would be for the best.

Chapter 9

Georgia ignored the grumbling from the man beside her as they strolled across the street toward Gracie's. He had a list of complaints as long as her arm. But she was determined he would not squash her excitement.

Except for a five-minute call to pass on her new telephone number and address, Celeste had not contacted her since the day her friend returned from her elopement. Several times Georgia had been tempted to drop by; however, realizing a new house did not come with instructions on how to take care of it, she decided to give her friend a chance to settle in before disturbing her.

Oblivious to the pedestrians who wanted to get by, William stopped in the middle of the sidewalk. "I don't see the purpose of us coming here."

The man was working on her last nerve. It wasn't like he had not been forewarned about the party. She had told him she planned on attending when he dropped by her apartment the previous evening to tell her they were going out the next night. At the time, he had agreed, but the strained smile on his face should have warned her he was not happy about her decision.

That evening, when he arrived to pick her up, he appeared surprised when she handed him a gift-wrapped box. She reminded him about the party, and his mumbled, "Yeah, right," indicated he had forgotten about it. She initially gave him the benefit of the doubt. Between his job, the work he was doing to make his presence known in the community, and the boys he mentored in the neighborhood, she could not expect him to remember everything. When he pointed his car in a direction opposite of Gracie's, she realized he was deliberately ignoring her wishes.

William finally saw the light as they stopped for a red light and Georgia opened the door to climb out of the car. When he demanded to know what she was doing, she stated she was going to the party if she had to walk there. She was certain his decision to back down had more to do with Pastor Peters and his wife pulling up next to them than with what she had said. It would not have looked good for him to have an argument in public. Georgia did not care about the reason behind his change of heart. Seeing her friend was all that mattered.

Taking his hand, Georgia walked up to the front of the club. Because of the party, the venue would be closed to the public. A doorman she had never seen before turned patrons away. She waited until the couple in front of her walked off before she stepped up to the door.

"Where do you think you're going?" the young man in the ill-fitted uniform asked when she reached for the door. With the pimples dotting his cheeks, he reminded her of a kid playing dress up.

"I'm here for the party."

His upper lip curled in disgust. Thanks to the lights in front of the building, she clearly saw the disbelief in his eyes. "I don't think so."

"Will you please get Mr. Santiano? He'll tell you I'm invited."

"Who?"

"Marco Santiano, the owner of Gracie's."

"Ain't no Santiano owns this club." The young man snorted. "Mr. Gianni Acardis is the owner."

"Then can you please get his wife."

"I don't answer to her. I only do what Mr. Acardis tells me to do. He said this was a private party. Only family allowed."

Georgia felt her heart break. The only explanation she could come up with for the exclusion was her big mouth. She had gone sixteen years without voicing her suspicions about Gianni. Why couldn't she have kept quiet?

William touched her arm. "Come on."

Despite the overwhelming urge to break down and bawl, she refused to let anyone see the tears in her eyes. Instead, she allowed him to lead her away from the club.

"And don't think about returning. No spades allowed."

Georgia froze. In all the years she'd visited the club, she never thought she would hear that vile statement.

"I'm not surprised," William mumbled.

She looked up and saw the mocking in his eyes.

"Your friend got her husband. She doesn't need her little doll to play with."

Georgia squared her shoulders and held her head high. "Never mention this night again."

The patronizing gleam in his eyes said he was happy she had been taken down a notch. She suspected he would not abide by her wishes never to speak of that night again. But, at that moment, he wisely kept his mouth shut as he waved her forward.

****

Nicholas did a double take at the brown coupe that cruised by. He would have sworn the woman in the passenger seat was Georgia. Yet that was impossible. It was Celeste's birthday. Georgia would head toward the club…not away from it.

As the car turned the corner, he squinted in an attempt to get a better look at the woman. She turned her head, and he noticed the single braid hanging between her shoulder blades. No, that was definitely not Georgia. She had stopped wearing braids when she started high school, claiming the hairstyle was too childish.

Figuring she was probably inside the club already, Nicholas put his convertible in park and stepped out of the car. He glanced around for the valet to get his keys. When no one stepped forward, he walked up to the door.

"The club's closed for a private party," a pimply-faced punk said.

"I'm aware of that. It's my sister's party."

"Let me check the guest list." The kid reached in his pocket and pulled out a wad of paper that looked like it had been pulled from the trash and stomped on several times before it had been crumpled into a ball. He unfurled the sheet and ran his finger down a list. "What's your name?"

Nicholas was too shocked to reply. Who the hell had put this kid at the door? He was not the greeter people would expect at a classy restaurant. A dive,

111

maybe…a slophouse, definitely…but not someplace that bore his mother's name.

Disgusted, Nicholas walked around the kid. He was reaching for the door when a large man stepped out from the shadows and into his path.

"He asked you a question."

Nicholas glanced up at the skyscraper with feet. The man folded beefy arms over a chest so wide that off-the-rack shirts could be considered a handkerchief.

The attempt to intimidate him nearly had Nicholas doubled over with laughter. Did the man really think he could not be taken down?

Nicholas did not have time to deal with either man. He needed to get inside and speak with Georgia. In the past, they'd had their share of arguments, but never anything that lasted more than two weeks like this one had.

Before he had the chance to demonstrate skills he had learned from years of watching over Georgia and Celeste, the door swung open and slapped the giant in the back. The man growled. His frown shifted to a leer as Celeste stepped outside.

She wore a sleeveless silver evening gown with a violet scarf around her neck. And, though Nicholas would agree she looked like a starlet, he did not appreciate the way the other man stared at her.

"Where have you been?" Celeste pushed past the big man in her way.

Nicholas shrugged out of his jacket and draped it over her shoulders.

"What are you doing? It's not that cold out here."

"I'm preventing a fight." He nodded toward the goon.

Celeste glanced up at her admirer and rolled her eyes. "Forget him." She turned back to Nicholas. "Where's Georgia?"

"I assumed she was here."

"How could she be? You just got here, Nicky."

"I figured her man would bring her."

"Georgia's not seeing anyone." Her eyes widened. "Is she?"

Nicholas took Celeste by the elbow and led her back inside Gracie's. The punk and the goon were too busy staring at a buxom blonde to harass them. He escorted her to the office, where they'd be able to talk without being disturbed.

Celeste sat on the edge of the sofa. "So, who's this guy Georgia's seeing?"

"Someone her father set her up with."

"You're wrong. She'd never go out with someone her father set her up with. He tried it once before, and the man bored her."

"There must be something about this guy. I've seen her with him more than once."

"When?"

"Two days after you ran off with Gianni. I'm surprised Georgia didn't tell you."

Celeste glanced at her hands in her lap. "We haven't actually spoken since right after I got back." Her voice was barely above a whisper.

Nicholas could not believe his ears. The two women had never gone that long without communicating. When Georgia visited her relatives in the country, Celeste and she wrote so many letters, posts were still being delivered days after Georgia returned.

"No, you're wrong." Celeste shook her head. "Georgia's at home, waiting for you to pick her up." She shot off the sofa. "I bet if you call her, she'll not only answer the phone, but she'll fuss at you for being late." She reached around him and picked up the handset. "Go ahead, call her."

Though Nicholas suspected otherwise, he prayed Celeste was right. Georgia fussing at him would be better than the alternative.

Nicholas reached back and dialed the number to the Collins apartment. As the dial rotated back to its original position, he took the handset his sister held to her chest.

After twenty rings, he shook his head. Celeste reached around him and disconnected the call.

"That doesn't mean anything. She's probably waiting for you in the bar."

Before she could beg him to, Nicholas dialed the number to the bar. The phone rang twice before he heard the murmur of voices rising to be heard over Sammy Davis Jr. "Sugar's." He recognized the voice of Raymond Torres, who tended bar part-time.

"May I speak to Georgia?"

"Hey, Nick. She left out of here an hour ago with her date."

"Did she say where she was going?"

"I overheard him mention a church social to her father."

"Okay, thanks."

"You want me to tell her you called?"

"No, I'll get in touch with her later."

Nicholas dropped the handset onto its base. He would never have thought Georgia would take her objection to Celeste's marriage that far. It was one thing to distance herself from Gianni, but another to turn her back on her friend.

"She's not coming, is she." Celeste's voice cracked. Her bottom lip trembled and tears gathered in her eyes.

Nicholas pulled his sister to his chest. The last time she had been that miserable was her sixth birthday party. She cared nothing about the elaborate celebration their father had planned or the expensive presents the guests had brought her. All she wanted was to spend the day with her friend.

He wanted to hate Georgia for the slight, but his heart could not let him. Instead, he needed to find a way to repair the rift in the relationship…for Celeste's sake and his.

Chapter 10

Everything about the house was wrong.

Nicholas's ears were not assaulted by high-pitched giggles. The aroma of spicy meats and sweet pastries did not drift from the kitchen. And bodies were not sprawled across the furniture. Instead, the scent of pine cleaner hung in the air, the tick from the second hand in the grandfather clock broke the silence, and the furniture was void of bodies that made the house a home.

He caught the door before it collided with the frame. A lively entrance felt out of place.

"Anyone home?" he called out as the door softly closed behind him.

"Who's there?" his father's voice drifted from upstairs.

He jogged up the steps, two at a time, to the second level, shared by his father and grandmother. He strolled down the carpet-lined hall and stopped on the threshold of the master bedroom.

"It's your son."

"I forgot I had children." The older man glanced at Nicholas's reflection in the mirror before refocusing his gaze on himself. "Happens when no one visits me for a month."

"I called you."

"A thirty-second 'Hey, Pops, just calling to see

what's up'? At least your sister has a good excuse. She's adjusting to marriage. But you—you'd think you could pull out and zip up long enough to visit your old man."

"I also work."

"Taking bets and breaking bones? When are you gonna get a real job?"

"When you do."

The older man faced him. "Don't look down your nose at what I do. I'm in the business of helping people."

"For twenty-five percent interest or fifty percent of the profits. Whatever's greater."

His father's eyes narrowed. "Watch it. I can still beat you."

Nicholas sighed. He woke up that morning feeling as if something was missing. Whenever he felt out of sorts, a trip to his childhood home brightened his mood. For the first time, however, it was not working. Instead of arguing with his father, he needed to get things back to normal.

"Listen, Pops, I'm here now. Why don't we go to the kitchen, and you can fix some sausage and peppers. I'll knock on Nonna's door and tell her you're cooking."

"You can knock all you want, but she won't answer." His father turned back to the mirror. "She went out with a couple of women from her church."

"So it'll be the two of us."

"No, it's just gonna be you. I'm going out."

Nicholas took in the other man's suit and for the first time recognized the aftershave his father only wore on special occasions.

"You're dressing kind of fancy for a poker game with the guys."

"I'm not playing tonight." He adjusted his tie. "I've got a date."

"You have a date?"

"Whaddaya think? I'm too old to go out?"

"No, I just never thought about you dating."

"There's nothing for you to think about. It's none of your business." His father reached for the jacket lying on the foot of his bed. "Instead of standing there interrogating me, why don't you go out there and find a decent dame and make an honest woman out of her?" He shook his head. "What am I asking? Why should I be lucky like James?"

A flash of red clouded Nicholas's vision. His father did not need to elaborate. He realized the older man was referring to the guy Georgia was seeing.

"By the way, do you know why Georgia missed your sister's party?"

As with his uncle, he did not want to discuss the woman. However, feeling he had already antagonized his father enough, he decided to give him the bare details.

"Georgia and I had a misunderstanding."

"Meaning someone said something he shouldn't." His father shrugged into his jacket, then turned back to the mirror to smooth the lines. "What did you say?"

"Why does it have to be my fault?" He hadn't been the one making accusations about others.

The visit was not turning out the way Nicholas had expected. Maybe he needed to take his father's advice…or at least part of it. He was not ready to marry, but he could find someone for the night.

After wishing the older man well, Nicholas drove to Gracie's. He hadn't been to the venue since Celeste's party two weeks earlier. Every time he thought about that night, he got heated. How could Georgia skip her friend's party? Even if she did not like Gianni, she could have avoided the man.

Nicholas had meant to confront Georgia about her slight. With Gianni no longer working with him, he could not easily get away during the day. By the time he was free, it was too late to visit her. Deciding the argument had gone on too long, he made a note to get to her apartment before she left for the diner in the morning.

Remembering the lack of valets during the birthday part, Nicholas parked in an empty spot around the corner from the club. After raising the top and locking the doors, he strolled back to the front.

"Where do you think you're going?" The goon who had confronted him outside the party stepped in front of the door.

Nicholas was getting annoyed. As he sized up the man to figure out the best way to bring him to his knees, the younger punk draped an arm around Nicholas's shoulders.

"It's all right. This is Nicholas Santiano. He's Mr. Acardi's brother-in-law."

Nicholas wasn't sure what bothered him most—the kid's chumminess or the stench from his uniform.

He plucked the punk's arm off his shoulder. He then reached for his wallet, pulled out a couple of bills, and shoved them into the kid's front pocket.

"Get that uniform cleaned." After a second, he shoved a couple more bills into the pocket. "Better yet, go get a uniform that fits."

The giant eyeballed the wallet. If he was expecting a tip, he had a long wait ahead of him. Nicholas sneered at the other man before he headed into the club.

Nicholas searched the crowd for Alton, but he did not see the familiar face. The stench of cheap cigars and perfume hung in the air. Instead of a melody from the house band, raunchy conversations and boisterous laughter echoed through the building.

Around the dining room, men who looked like they would be more comfortable ogling a performance at a two-bit dive knocked back drinks. The women with them looked like the type he'd pick up outside the dive…for a price.

Across the room, Gianni stood by the bar talking to a man who had probably seen better days a decade earlier. His hand shook as he held it out. Gianni slid one palm over it. His other hand slipped into the man's coat.

The man nodded as he stepped back from the bar. With a smile, Gianni patted the man's shoulder. He then turned to the bar and passed the bartender the wad of cash he had taken out of the other man's hand. As he spoke, a young woman Nicholas had gone out with several times moved to Gianni's side. She leaned toward him and whispered in his ear.

Gianni completed his conversation, then turned in Nicholas's direction. He held out his hands and maneuvered around the tables.

"What brings you by?" Gianni grasped Nicholas's hand and pulled him into a quick embrace.

"Figured I'd stop by and hang a bit."

"Come, have a drink." He draped a hand on Nicholas's shoulder and led him to the bar.

Nicholas spotted the man he'd had a confrontation with at his grandmother's party. A woman who was nearly hanging out of the top of her dress was draped over him. This was not the same club where they'd celebrated his Nonna's birthday or where he'd teased Georgia as he held her close to him on the dance floor.

"The place looks different." Nicholas did not recognize any of the staff. "Where's Alton?"

"Things didn't work out. But, you know…that's how things go."

Nicholas wasn't so sure. As far as he knew, Alton got along with everyone. That's what made the man good at his job. He could charm a disgruntled customer into being his best friend.

"What's the deal with the goon outside?"

"Relax." Gianni rapped his fist on the bar. "Give him a shot of the good stuff."

The bartender placed a glass on the bar and poured the drink. Nicholas saluted him with the glass, then threw back his drink.

Tears formed in his eyes. He was certain turpentine was better than what he had been served. If that was the good stuff, what the hell was his friend serving to the customers?

"This is not what Pops intended when he opened the club," Nicholas said once he regained the ability to speak.

"Your old man didn't have the vision. A few changes and I've got this place packed and a line of people outside waiting to get in." Gianni reached to his right and grasped a bottle. He poured the amber liquid into a glass, then knocked back his drink.

"How's Celeste?"

"She's doing good. Settling into married life. She's doing fine keeping house, and she's okay in the kitchen, but she's still got a lot to learn in the bedroom."

Nicholas nearly swallowed his tongue. "That's my sister you're talking about." There was some information about Celeste he didn't need to know.

"You forget she's a married woman. No more blushing bride." Gianni reached behind him for the woman who had been at his side when Nicholas walked into the club. "Speaking of someone who won't be blushing on her wedding night, you remember Alice."

Up close, Nicholas quickly remembered what he had seen in Alice. Her low-cut blouse could barely contain the assets that made men drool, and her narrow skirt hugged long legs he had enjoyed spending time between.

"Hey, Nicky." Her low, breathy voice reminded him of a woman panting through an orgasm. The thought woke a body part that had not received the attention it deserved for a long while. It also reminded him of one of the reasons he had shown up at the club. "It's been a long time."

He leered back at her, enjoying the view. "Yeah, too long."

"How've you been?"

"I've been in search of some companionship tonight," he confessed.

"And Alice was telling me she wanted some attention." Gianni patted their shoulders. "Why don't you two enjoy a round of drinks on me while you get reacquainted?"

After a quick nod to the bartender, Gianni rushed away and met a man halfway across the room. The new arrival sniffled and wiped his nose with the back of his hand. He exchanged a few words with the club owner before Gianni led him toward the kitchen. Two large men followed them out of the room.

The encounter piqued Nicholas's curiosity. However, a bold move by Alice convinced him to stay out of his friend's business. The club had been given to Gianni as a wedding present since Nicholas never wanted any part of it. Therefore, who was he to butt into its affairs?

Chapter 11

The date was a failure.

At the diner, William had taken the liberty of ordering a BLT that Georgia could barely finish without gagging. Afterwards, they went to a double feature. Having purchased the tickets in advance, he rushed her into the theater. It wasn't until she was settled in the center of the row that she discovered what was playing. Not wanting to disturb the other moviegoers, she remained for the show.

"Woman, I don't believe you're coppin' an attitude over the movies," William grumbled.

When others were around, William was well spoken. He corrected the boys he mentored, telling them people were not only judged by the color of their skin but also by how they walked and talked. Lately, whenever it was just the two of them, he spoke like one of the creeps who hung out on the street corner, as if she wasn't worth the effort to maintain appearances.

"I told you I don't like movies with killing. Geesh, I don't think I'll ever sleep again after that second movie."

"How was I supposed to know you wouldn't like *The Last Train from Gun Hill* or *The Man Who Could Cheat Death*?"

"I told you when you asked me about it last week. Come to think of it, I also told you I don't like BLTs.

You did everything without taking any of my feelings into consideration. How'd you like it if I ordered you a fried egg sandwich and made you sit through *The Five Pennies*?"

"Not gonna happen. My dime, my say."

"Is that so?" Georgia's eyes narrowed. "In that case, next time I'll pay for my own ticket."

"Come on, sugar, don't be that way."

"Why not? I don't have a problem paying my own way. In fact, you don't even need to pick me up. I'll take the bus."

"Don't be like that." He grabbed her arm as she turned to the door. "You know I don't like it when you're upset."

"From the way you were acting tonight, I didn't think you gave two hoots about me."

"You know that's not true. I wouldn't be by every night if I didn't care." He released her arm and reached up to stroke her cheek. "Listen, don't you ever doubt my feelings for you."

His eyes dropped from her eyes to her mouth, cuing her in on what was about to happen. Despite Celeste's insistence that men wanted her, Georgia had few experiences with the opposite sex. She had only been kissed once before.

Her curiosity overrode her anger. She decided she wanted to go for it. Not wanting to appear too eager or easy, she waited until he leaned forward and pressed his lips against hers.

Even with her limited knowledge, she knew she should have felt something more than the need to simply tolerate his mouth on hers. Where were the quivers she read about in romance novels? She did not feel the slightest thrill when his lips moved against hers or when he slipped his tongue past her lips. The act was as exciting as being served liver after dreaming of steak.

William leaned in to deepen the kiss. It felt like he was trying to suck the breath out of her. When her head became light and her lungs were about to burst, she pulled back and placed her hands on his chest.

To her relief, he backed off. William dropped back in his seat and panted like an overheated dog. "Damn," he gasped.

Georgia also sat back, but she did not feel the same sentiment. Maybe she had done something wrong?

William shifted in his seat. In the streetlight, she saw the lust in the man's eyes. He was ready for round two. Celeste, however, could think of plenty of other things that would be more exciting...scrubbing the kitchen floor was one of them.

Deciding she needed to get out of there before he saw hope where there was none, she grabbed for the door handle. "I better get inside, before Daddy steps out to see why we've been sitting in this car so long," she said.

As she expected, William moved in the opposite direction. He had an equal amount of respect for and fear of her father and would not do anything that would make her scream for his mentor.

"Wait there."

William climbed out of the car and jogged around to the passenger side.

"How 'bout we drive up to Harlem and hit the Savoy tomorrow night?" he asked as he opened her door.

"I'll have to get back to you." While she enjoyed hanging out at the ballroom in Harlem, after this evening she had to reconsider going out with him again.

Georgia accepted his hand and stepped out of the car. He kicked the door closed. With his hand on her back, he escorted her to the bar and opened the door. She walked in—and stopped short.

"What the…Daddy?"

The radio that normally sat on the end of the bar lay smashed on the floor. Tables were overturned and the chairs scattered around the room. Broken bottles lay on the shelves behind the bar. Liquor and the contents of ashtrays littered the floor.

There was the occasional fight at the bar, if someone didn't appreciate another's tone of voice or someone caught her man looking at another woman. Maybe a drink was spilt or a chair was overturned. There was never damage to the extent of what she was surveying.

"Daddy?" Georgia called out again.

Silence answered her.

Her heart pounded as she stepped over glasses and other debris. She moved toward the back room, her fear growing with each step she took. She reached the door and pushed. An object blocked it from swinging more than a foot.

Georgia squeezed through the opening. Her hand shook as she reached up and pulled the string to the overhead light. A dim glow illuminated the body blocking the door.

**** 

Nicholas flopped back onto the bed, letting his arm fall over his eyes. Despite trying everything, he was unable to complete the task.

It was a first for him. He had never had a problem in bed. Yet even Alice's skillful mouth did not help matters.

Mentally, Nicholas had been ready when they left the club. He had not complained when Alice started the foreplay during the drive. It was one less thing they'd have to do when they reached her apartment.

Once inside, they did not bother turning on the lights. Using the wall as their guide, they felt their way from the door to her bedroom, leaving a trail of clothes in the hall. But the moment they crossed the threshold, his body stopped responding to her stimulation. With each stroke she made, his body recoiled until it was soft and unmoving.

"I don't know what's up." Nicholas groaned.

"It's definitely not you," Alice replied.

He glared at her, despite the veil of darkness that hid the expression.

"That's not funny."

"Oh, lighten up." She shoved his shoulder. "It happens."

The snicker that accompanied the statement offered him little comfort. She was never going to let him live it down. Hell, she'd probably have announcements in every New York paper by morning.

Nicholas sat up and swung his legs over the side of the bed. He reached for the boxers he had shed before diving onto the bed.

"What are you doing?"

"Cutting out. It's obvious nothing's going to happen here tonight."

"That's not necessary." Alice switched on the lamp

next to her. "There's other things we could do." She pulled a bag of white powder from the drawer to the nightstand.

Nicholas jerked back from the substance. He had been called a lot of things—criminal, thug, skirt chaser, and jerk—but no one had ever been able to call him a doper.

In order to handle his businesses, he needed to think straight. All it would take was one lapse in judgment and he'd lose everything—his money, his family, his freedom…his life.

He also stayed clear of anyone who did drugs. If they weren't hustling for money, they were stealing or snitching to get their next fix.

Nicholas stood and yanked up his boxers. "What are you using that for?"

"It's no big deal."

"That stuff will mess up your mind."

He walked around to her side of the bed and snatched the bag from her.

"What are you doing?" She reached for the bag.

He stepped out of her reach. "Getting rid of this."

"Don't you dare!" she screamed as he walked out of the room. "Come back here!"

Ignoring her unholy screeches, he ducked into the bathroom and locked the door. He lifted the toilet lid and seat, opened the bag, and poured out the contents. Alice's screams switched to curses when he depressed the lever. She punched and kicked the door.

Taking advantage of his location, Nicholas relieved himself. After washing his hands, he opened the door.

Alice shoved past him. She picked up the empty bag from the floor, glanced at the clear water in the bowl, and screamed.

"Asshole." She charged at him, striking his chest with her fists. "Get out."

"With pleasure."

Nicholas started up the hall, gathering his clothes along the way. He stopped in the foyer, pulled on his pants, and slipped his feet into his loafers. With the rest of his clothes under his arm, he yanked open the door.

Gianni stood in the hall, his fist raised to knock.

"What do you want?" Alice screamed.

Gianni glanced at the naked, irate woman and then at his partially clothed friend. "I take it I'm interrupting something."

"You can't interrupt something he couldn't start."

"*Chiudi la bocca!*" Nicholas waved her off.

She should consider herself lucky he had been raised not to hit a woman. He was certain another man would not have brushed off her comment regarding his lack of performance. Instead of telling her to shut her mouth, someone else would have done it for her.

"*Cagna,*" he cursed as he stepped into the hall. He may not have believed in hitting a woman, but he had no problem calling a bitch a bitch.

She countered with, "*Bastardo,*" before slamming the door behind him.

"What was that about?" Gianni asked.

"Did you know she's into drugs?"

Gianni shrugged his shoulders, which was not the response Nicholas would have expected from his friend. Their lessons on the evils of narcotics had been accompanied by a threat of what Nicholas's father would do if he ever caught them using, dealing, or hanging around with anyone involved with drugs.

"Your old man called the club. You're to meet him at Wyckoff Heights."

Nicholas's heart skipped a beat. Since his father was searching for him, it was obvious the older man was not in the hospital. Gianni was too calm for it to be Celeste. That only left his grandmother.

He dropped his jacket and tie on the floor and shoved one arm into his shirt.

"What happened?"

"That chick who's always hanging around Celeste…"

"Georgia? What about her?"

"Someone busted up her father's bar and attacked the old man."

Nicholas froze with his shirt half on. His fear switched to Georgia. She had been a part of his life for sixteen years. Even the falling out could not diminish his concern for her.

"Was she hurt?"

"Your old man didn't say."

Nicholas finished pulling his shirt on and grabbed the rest of his things.

"Thanks." He slapped his friend's shoulder as he rushed past him.

He was thankful for the late hour and few drivers on the road. With his foot on the gas and a disregard for traffic lights, Nicholas raced to the hospital. Despite his erratic driving, he arrived at his destination outside an ambulance.

Nicholas rushed into the building and past the nurse at the front desk. Following the signs, he raced down the hall toward the waiting room. As he stepped into the room, every head inside turned toward him, but he focused solely on Georgia.

She stared back at him, her brow wrinkled and her lips pursed tight. She had twisted the strap to her purse into a knot. Dust and blood covered the front of her dress.

For years he had protected her from bullies, celebrated her accomplishments, and mourned her losses. He therefore assumed she would want him to sit with her while she waited on news of her father. However, the lack of emotion in her eyes made him wonder whether his presence was welcome.

It took less than five seconds for him to take in everything, and it felt like hours had passed before Georgia sprang out of her chair. Her bag fell to the floor as she rushed across the room. When she reached him, his arms wrapped around her and held her close.

Nicholas wanted to tell her everything would be all right, but having no more information about her father, he would have been feeding her a line. He had never done so in the past and was not about to start. He would simply hold her, offering as much comfort as his presence could provide.

Georgia laid her head on his chest. Nicholas regretted not going after her sooner. He missed their friendship…missed having her there to talk to…missed teasing her…and, most importantly, he simply missed having her around.

For a minute, no one and nothing else mattered. Though it had taken an unfortunate incident to return things to the way they should be, Georgia was back in his life, and he would do whatever it took to keep her there.

A throat cleared. Nicholas glanced over Georgia's

head at her date. The dust and blood on the other man's shirt indicated he had been with her when she found her father.

The other man stood, frowning, obviously not pleased someone else was holding his woman. Nicholas couldn't give a crap.

"In the hall," his father said, ending the staring contest.

Nicholas reluctantly released Georgia. He felt empty inside without her closeness.

"Thank you for coming." Her voice was void of emotion.

"I'll be back." Nicholas kissed her forehead before following his father out of the room.

Unwilling to let her out of his sight, he stood just outside the door. She shuffled back to her chair and sat. Her companion towered over her. In angry whispers, he appeared to question her. She stared straight ahead until he gave up and sat next to her.

"You look like a bum," his father said. "Fix your clothes."

Nicholas glanced at the man who never left the house in anything other than a full suit. His jacket was missing, as was his tie, and the top two buttons of his shirt were open.

Considering the situation, Nicholas felt it would be best to keep all comments regarding his father's appearance to himself. Instead, he focused on his own disheveled clothing. With no concern over who would walk by, he unbuttoned the shirt.

"How is he?"

"He was unconscious when they brought him in," his father replied. "They just wheeled him to surgery."

"Does Georgia know who did this?"

"I didn't ask, but I have my suspicions."

Nicholas nodded as he opened his pants and tucked in his shirt. Knowing his father, the older man had spoken to Mr. Collins after learning about the previous break-in at the bar. And, while Georgia's father, believing he could handle everything on his own, may not have said anything, Nicholas's father would have asked around to at least get the name of the person attempting to intimidate the business owner.

"I have a few things I need to take care of. Stay with Georgia."

It was a needless command. Nicholas had no intention of leaving her side.

Again he chose to keep his comments to himself. He simply nodded as he refastened his pants. He headed into the waiting room and sat in the row of seats across the room from Georgia and the man with her.

Nicholas pulled out a pack of cigarettes. He lit one, took a drag, and then sat back and watched Georgia.

Lost in thought, she did not reintroduce him to her companion. Not that Nicholas gave a fig. The only thing he wanted to know was why the other man had to sit so close to her. There were perfectly good seats…in the lobby.

**** 

The thunderous sound of soft-soled shoes slapping against the marble broke the silence. Georgia sat up and listened, her hopes rising as each step grew louder.

The doctor stepped into the room. Georgia jumped out of her seat, jostling William awake. Nicholas, who had not slept, was by her side when she reached the doctor.

"Your father's out of surgery," the doctor announced.

Georgia let out the breath she had been holding. As long as her worst fear did not come true, she was certain she could handle whatever else he had to tell her.

"He took quite a beating, and he was stabbed several times. He'll have a long recovery ahead of him."

"When can I see him?"

"We're getting him settled in a ward—"

"He's getting a private room," Nicholas stated.

"I was under the assumption…well, you know…" the doctor stuttered.

"What?"

The doctor glanced from William to Georgia. "A private room can get expensive. How do you plan to pay for it?"

"You worry about the doctoring," Nicholas said. "I'll worry about the expense."

The doctor glared at Nicholas for a second before he nodded his head.

"When can I see him?" Georgia repeated.

"Right now, he's resting, so I suggest you go home and do the same. Come back in the morning, during visiting hours."

"Excuse me, Doctor, you have a patient," a nurse announced from the doorway.

"I'll be right there," he called over his shoulder, before addressing the group in front of him. "If you'll excuse me."

William let out a low whistle once the doctor had rushed out of the room. "That's a relief. For a while I

135

was wondering. He was a mess when we found him." He glanced at his watch. "It's been a long night. I'll be lucky if I get two hours of sleep after I drop you off."

Georgia shook her head. "I'm not going anywhere."

"What are you talking about? The doctor told you to go home."

"I don't care what he said. I'm not going anywhere till I see my father."

"Why? It's not like you're a doctor or anything."

"I'm not leaving."

William released a hard breath. His attitude reminded her of their earlier discussion.

"I don't have time for this, woman. I have to go to work in the mornin'."

"Then leave." Nicholas's tone was calm, yet the challenge was clear. "If Georgia wants to stay, then she stays."

"I'm her ride."

"I can drive her home."

William cocked an eyebrow. Georgia knew he was facing a dilemma. And, no matter the choice he made, he would not come out ahead. If he left, he'd look like a cold-hearted bastard. If he stayed, he'd look like a punk caving in to a woman.

Understanding his situation and caring were two different things. She was not in the mood to soothe egos. Her only concern was her father. She was not going to leave the hospital until she saw him. Even if it meant she had to walk home.

"William, just go."

He jerked back, apparently shocked by her order. He opened his mouth, yet one glance over her head had him pursing his lips. Georgia did not know what Nicholas did to change the other man's mind, but, at the moment, she was grateful for any help.

"You sure?" William asked through clenched teeth.

"Yes."

"Fine." He leaned forward, his lips aiming for hers.

Georgia turned her head. The kiss landed on her cheek. She refused let him mark his territory by kissing her in front of Nicholas. The only person in the hospital who should be playing with tonsils was the doctor.

"So it's like that," he whispered in her ear.

"This is not the time or the place," Georgia replied before she stepped back from him. "We'll talk later."

William straightened and muttered, "Sure, later." Without acknowledging Nicholas, he turned and strolled out.

As the sound of his wingtips tapping against marble faded, Georgia spun to face Nicholas. Realizing Mr. Santiano would want to know about her father, Georgia had contacted him after calling an ambulance. She had not been surprised when he walked into the waiting room seconds after she and William got there. But she had been shocked when she looked up and saw Nicholas in the doorway an hour later.

Georgia had been certain that revealing her suspicions about Gianni had ended their friendship. However, he had proven he was a true friend by not letting their disagreement keep him from being there for her in a time of need.

"Thank you for coming," she said. "You don't have to stay."

He reached for her hand and held it tight. "Yes, I do." His tone was firm, telling her there would be no more discussion regarding the matter. As long as she needed him, he would be by her side.

Chapter 12

The nurse shook her head. She muttered a snide remark about the stubbornness of some people before she walked away. Georgia did not give the other woman a second glance. She sat in the lone chair in the private room. As promised, Nicholas remained by her side.

After two hours of prodding, the hospital personnel had finally stopped insisting Georgia and Nicholas go home. They let them sit in the waiting room until visiting hours. A doctor then escorted them to the room where her father slept.

Georgia spent the day by her father's side, watching him sleep. Several times he regained consciousness and muttered a few incoherent words before drifting off again.

Nicholas thought about her loyalty. Someone willing to trade her comfort to stay by another's side would not allow an argument to keep her from a friend. She would have tried long before this to bury the hatchet and find some way to make things work. So there had to be another explanation for her missing Celeste's party.

"I had a feeling I'd find you here." His father stepped into the room. He walked around the bed and stopped by Georgia. "You look like hell."

The corners of her lips did not quite make it into

the grin she tried to force onto her face. Her brow wrinkled and her eyes drooped. A nurse had given her a rubber band to contain her hair, though without a comb she could not do anything about the tangles. Strands that had not made it into the ponytail stuck out in various directions from her head.

Of course, she looked better than the man lying in the bed. The left side of her father's face was swollen. A bruise surrounded his left eye, his nose was twice its normal size, and his lip was busted. A cast covered his right arm and a splint held together the pointer and middle finger on his left hand. The bulge from the bandage by his left ribs indicated the location of one of his stab wounds.

"You shouldn't worry so, *cara*." His father reached out and stroked her cheek. "Everything's all right."

Georgia glanced into his father's eyes. A silent exchange followed, and after a few seconds, she nodded. "Thank you," she said softly.

"Anytime." The man dropped his hand to his side. "I want you to go home and rest. Someone will call you when James wakes."

She sighed.

He glanced over her head. "Drive her home."

Nicholas stubbed out his cigarette in the ashtray next to him. He hopped off the windowsill, walked over to the chair, and held out his hand.

Georgia looked from his hand to the bed and then back. After a second, she slipped her hand into his and allowed him to pull her from the chair. She leaned over the bed's railing and placed a kiss on her father's head.

Nicholas's father slapped him on the back before dropping into the chair Georgia had vacated. He sat back, rested his elbows on the arms of the chair, and folded his hands. His shirt sleeves were folded back to his elbows. Around the cuff, spots of blood stained the white material.

Nicholas held Georgia's hand as he escorted her to the elevators. As they stood waiting, another nurse walked by, noticed the intimacy between the two, and frowned. With his middle finger, he scratched the side of his nose, and she walked off in a huff.

Georgia reached up, laid her free hand over his, and gently pushed his appendage down. She then pulled him into the elevator, which had arrived during the quiet exchange.

****

Georgia ignored the glares and sneers from those they passed in the lobby. She could care less whether or not people approved of her holding hands with Nicholas.

It had been him, not them, who had waited by her side through the night to see her father. By staying, he, not they, had shown her what it meant to be a true friend. Therefore, it was only his, not their, opinion that mattered to her.

Without a word, they walked to his car. Nicholas drove for three blocks toward her apartment before he made a sudden turn. Trusting him, Georgia sat back as he moved farther and farther away from her residence.

Nicholas finally parked in front of the Santiano home. He used the shortcut of hopping to the back and then out of the car to reach the sidewalk. He opened the door for Georgia, took her hand, and helped her out.

As before, he did not release her once she was on her feet. He held her hand as he escorted her through the garden entrance.

"Nonna, we're home," Nicholas called out as he pushed the door closed behind them.

The older woman rushed out of the kitchen with her arms out. Georgia let go of Nicholas and moved into the woman's embrace. Sophie Santiano had been as much a grandmother for her as she had been for her children's children. And Georgia knew she could always depend on the other woman for comfort.

"How's your father?"

Georgia pulled back and shook her head. "He was still sleeping when we left."

"Evil. That was nothing but pure evilness. I hope the ones responsible rot in hell."

"I'm sure they are."

Sophie brushed a stray lock of hair from Georgia's brow. "You don't look good. You need to rest."

"I have to take care of some things first."

"Psst. Whatever you have to take care of can wait." She grabbed Georgia's wrist and dragged her toward the kitchen. "First you'll eat. Then you'll rest."

Georgia glanced over her shoulder and mouthed, "Coward," to Nicholas. She suspected he wanted her to do the same but knew she would've argued with him had he made the suggestion. He therefore brought her to his grandmother, knowing she would never argue with the older woman.

His grimace shifted to a smirk. Instead of following the women, he turned toward the stairs.

Sophie released Georgia's arm when they reached the table, while she continued toward the stove, picked up the wooden spoon, and pointed to a chair. Obeying the unspoken command, Georgia plopped down.

"How will you manage until your father's better?"

"I just have to clean the bar, and then I'll be able to open again."

"You remember, if you need any help—"

"I'll call Mr. Santiano," Georgia insisted, though things would have to be really bad before she did so. Her father was a proud man and would consider any financial assistance a handout.

"Good girl."

Georgia watched as the woman fussed over each pot on the stove. She always timed everything so the entire meal was ready at the same time. One dish did not have a chance to get cold or dry out as she waited for another to finish. She had tried to teach Celeste the same skill, but her granddaughter was more concerned about thumbing through fashion magazines than she was about doing anything in the kitchen. She figured whatever instruction she needed she'd get from a cookbook after she was married.

Georgia wondered how successful the lessons were. She had tried following a recipe in a cookbook once, and though the meal was edible, it was merely okay.

Nicholas entered the kitchen as his grandmother drained the pasta. He carried a snifter with a generous amount of what she assumed was brandy sloshing around inside.

"Nicholas, set the table," his grandmother ordered. "Georgia, go freshen up."

Georgia stood as Nicholas placed the glass in front of the chair across from where she had been sitting. She shuffled into the bathroom a few steps from the kitchen and closed the door.

Not in the mood to see her reflection in the mirror over the sink, she ignored the overhead light. She already knew her hair was disheveled and her clothes were dirty and she felt grimy.

She washed her hands and dried them on one of the two navy blue hand towels that hung on the rack by the door. When she returned to the kitchen, a plate of fish, pasta with sauce, and bread sat on the table in front of her chair.

"I can't eat this." She slipped into the chair. "You made it for yourself."

"You eat it. I'll have chicken."

"But—"

"You should know better than to argue with Nonna," Nicholas said. "You never win."

Georgia frowned.

"Don't tease her, Nicky," his grandmother scolded as she added a chicken breast to the pan in which she had fried the fish. "Though he is right. Now, sit down, *carina*, and eat."

Georgia sighed before slipping back into her chair. Nicholas sat across from her and sipped his brandy as she took a bite.

"Speaking of fish," the older woman said, "I had a dream about one last night."

Georgia swallowed the bite she had taken. "It's not me."

"Of course not."

"What's going on?" Nicholas asked.

"If you dream about fish, that means someone you know is pregnant," his grandmother replied. "A colored woman in my women's group told me that."

Nicholas shook his head. "You don't believe that,

do you?"

"Why not? Just 'cause you're not raised on something, it doesn't mean you can't respect someone else's belief." The woman placed another plate of fish in front of Nicholas. "Now, eat up."

Though Georgia would not admit it out loud, the meal hit the spot. It gave her the energy she would need to tackle the mess at the bar. After she cleaned, she would need to take inventory. She hoped there was enough liquor to get them to Monday, when she could place an order.

"Thank you for the food, Nonna."

"Anytime, my dear." The older woman removed the empty plate from the table. "Now you'll go rest?"

"Yes," she said aloud, while mentally adding, "once I finish working."

\*\*\*\*

Nicholas flinched as he read the not-so-ladylike thoughts going through Georgia's mind.

Knowing she would go straight to the bar to clean up once he dropped her off, he drove toward his apartment after they left his father's house. The moment she realized they were driving in a direction away from her residence, she glared daggers at him. However, the fact she did not verbalize her thoughts indicated how tired she was.

Once the elevator reached the fourth floor, she silently followed him down the carpeted hall to the apartment. It had been four years since the first and only time she'd visited him.

She had showed up on the night of her senior prom with an intoxicated Celeste, begged him to provide his sister a safe place to sleep, and insisted he keep the incident from his father, who would have placed his daughter under lock and key until she was thirty, had he found out.

That night, Nicholas gave the girls his bed and slept on the sofa that was a foot too short for him. In the morning, he had a crick in his neck and a foul mood he took out on the young man who got his sister drunk.

Though he was aware of the consequences of the sleeping arrangements, he planned to turn over his bed to Georgia. He led her past the kitchen and bathroom to the bedroom.

Georgia glanced longingly at the bed. Her eyelids drooped, and Nicholas knew she was fighting an internal battle. She wanted to sleep, while at the same time she felt an obligation to take care of the bar for her father.

He reached forward and pushed one corner of her lips up. "Stop frowning. It's unbecoming."

She slapped his hand away. "If you don't like my frown, take me home where you won't have to look at it."

"If I do, you'll go straight to the bar and start cleaning up."

"I need to get the bar open as soon as possible. It's bad enough that it'll be closed tonight. Friday's one of our busiest nights."

"Look, if you're concerned about the money—"

"Don't you dare finish that sentence."

Her frown deepened, just like her father's would, at the suggestion of taking money from someone. The only difference was her lips were full and inviting, practically begging for someone to kiss them.

Nicholas mentally slapped himself. Georgia was

not like the women he took to bed. She was not to be used to satisfy his momentary desires and then forgotten about until he had another itch.

"It won't hurt you to stay one night." He opened the closet door and began rummaging through the clothes to get his mind away from the inappropriate thoughts he had been about to entertain. "I think there's a dress in here you can wear in the morning."

"You've got some nerve, giving me something another woman wore."

"It belongs to Celeste," Nicholas explained, suspecting she assumed one of his women had left the dress in his closet.

Aside from Celeste and her, no one had ever been invited into his bedroom. And Georgia was the only female not related to him who'd been allowed to step over the threshold of his apartment.

All his encounters occurred at the woman's apartment, and he always left by sunrise. A few women had been put off by his behavior, yet he found it necessary to ensure no one took the relationship too seriously.

He found the yellow dress in the back of the closet and pulled it out. "She left this in my hamper the last time she was here. I sent it to the laundry with my clothes."

"That's my dress." Georgia placed her hands on her hips. "I've been looking everywhere for it."

"You know better than to turn your back on Celeste when she's around your closet."

"I don't know why. Her clothes are more expensive than mine. I have to get my dresses on sale, or make 'em."

Nicholas held up the dress. "She must think you have more talent than the ones who design her clothes."

Georgia yawned widely, obviously too tired to remember her manners and cover her mouth. Shaking his head, Nicholas hung the dress back in the closet. He opened the fourth drawer in the six-drawer dresser and pulled out a pair of blue-striped pajamas.

"You can wear these." When Georgia made no move to take the nightclothes from him, he added, "I'm sure a hot shower would hit the spot."

With a sigh, Georgia snatched the pajamas from him and marched from the room. He followed her and stopped in front of the linen closet across from the bathroom. He passed her a washcloth and towel before grabbing a set of blue sheets.

"Do you mind if I use your detergent?"

Nicholas passed her the box of soap sitting on the floor of the closet.

While Georgia took advantage of the shower, he changed his sheets. Afterwards, he retreated to the living room and dropped onto the sofa. The cushions were comfortable enough to lounge on while watching television, but they were murder on his back when he slept on them.

Besides the night of her prom, Celeste invaded his sanctuary whenever Georgia made her annual trip down south to visit relatives. No sooner had her friend boarded the bus than his sister would be at his door claiming she was lonely. Last time, she had stayed the entire two weeks and his back had protested so fiercely he had considered asking his grandmother to help him pick out a sofa bed. However, when he finally had the time to go shopping, Celeste had married and he figured her sleeping-over days were over.

As he considered the benefits of sleeping on the floor, the bathroom door opened. The hinges to the linen closet creaked. He appreciated her consideration in returning the detergent. Though his apartment was not eat-off-the-bathroom-floor clean, he did not like to have anything out of place.

A moment later, Georgia leaned over the back of the sofa and stuck her head in his face. Her damp hair was pulled back into a single braid. Her skin smelled of his deodorant soap.

"Did you want to check behind my ears before you sent me to bed?"

Nicholas could think of a few things he wanted to do behind her ears—inhaling her fresh fragrance, licking her still damp skin, and kissing the spot until she sighed. He was beginning to feel the effects of her presence on his body, and he needed to get her away from him before he gave in to temptation.

He reached up and mussed her hair like he used to do when she was younger. As he expected, she pulled back and stood behind him. He peered down at his lap. To his relief, the effect of her presence was not noticeable.

"Did you want anything before you go to bed?" He dropped his head back to look at her.

She shook her head as she tried to stifle a yawn and failed. Once she finished sucking in air, she leaned down and placed a kiss on his nose.

"Thanks for everything."

"You know I'll always be there for you."

"I do now," Georgia said before she walked out of the living room.

Once the bedroom door clicked shut, he stood. He was sporting the hard-on Alice had been unable to coax from him the previous evening. With no one else available to help him, he needed to take matters into his own hands.

Nicholas stepped into the bathroom and flipped on the light. He groaned at the sight of the matching red lace bra and panties hanging across the shower rod.

It was going to be a long night.

Chapter 13

Nicholas paused in the doorway. In the window sat Georgia, the moonlight illuminating shapely legs barely covered by her pajama top. The pajama bottoms were folded neatly in a chair in the corner behind her. The memory of where her panties were hanging caused a return of the problem he had taken care of five hours earlier.

Georgia made no move to cover her legs. She rested her head against the window frame to stare outside.

Nicholas told his libido to settle down before he walked across the room to her.

"You should be sleeping."

"I should be tending bar right now." Her somber tone cut through him. He had never been able to stand to see her sad.

He hooked a finger under her chin and turned her face toward him. "The business will be all right if the bar's closed one more night."

"Daddy worked so hard to open the bar. I can't sit by and watch his dreams die." Her gaze dropped to her folded hands where they rested on her bent knees.

She was a rare person. There weren't too many people willing to work overtime for someone else's dream, especially when they weren't allowed to share in that dream. Because of her personality, he was determined to make her goals his.

He placed his hand over hers and squeezed. "His dream won't die."

Georgia lifted her head, and his eyes dropped to her lips. He remembered the last time she had stayed at his apartment.

Celeste and Georgia had been looking forward to their proms, as they had made pacts to get their first kiss that night. His sister's date, however, had made a pact with his friends to get a lot further.

Though the high school they attended was integrated, the colored students were encouraged to remain to one side of the gymnasium during the prom. With no close friends to look out for her, Celeste's date had been able to spike her drinks. Thankfully, her inability to hold her liquor had her fleeing from the room within an hour of their arrival, which alerted Georgia that something was amiss.

Once Celeste finished emptying the contents of her stomach on the floor of the ladies' room, Georgia had her date drive them to Nicholas's apartment. She then helped her friend get settled in the queen-sized bed before sitting on the windowsill to mourn her lost opportunity.

Feeling sorry for her, Nicholas had decided to make her fantasy come true. After telling her to close her eyes, he pressed his lips against hers.

Georgia had frozen, though he suspected it was due to her inexperience, not fear. He was gentle as he tasted the lingering sweetness of fruit punch and felt her soft lips.

The kiss was not magical. Nicholas did not see stars or feel the earth move. If he had been trying to get aroused, the kiss would not have done the job. However, when he pulled back, Georgia smiled as if it had been the most incredible experience of her life.

Her reaction had been silly, yet he did not laugh. She had been too innocent to know the difference. He figured once she married she'd learn what it truly felt like to be kissed.

Nicholas smiled as he remembered the kiss. It was the logical solution to his problem. It had worked once in suppressing his libido; surely it would work again.

So as not to startle her, he slowly leaned forward and pressed his lips against hers. As he expected, Georgia froze. Her reaction was the perfect turnoff. He could not get excited when a woman did nothing. He needed her to be an active participant before he could move forward.

Just as he felt the effects of her lack of participation, Georgia tilted her head to the side. Her mouth opened. The tip of her tongue swiped across his bottom lip.

Nicholas's eyes popped open. That was not a move from an inexperienced girl. It was a gesture made from a woman who knew how to turn a man on…and it was working. A surge flowed straight to the body part he had been trying to get flaccid.

\*\*\*\*

Georgia did not know what she was doing.

The two times she had been kissed, the men had taken the initiative. She only knew how to get a man to back off, something she did not want Nicholas to do.

For the first time since finding her father, she did not see the image of his battered body. Nicholas had distracted her and, though it would only be for a short time, she wanted to relish the peace.

Nicholas tensed. Believing she did something wrong and needed to quit before she repulsed him, Georgia pulled back. However, instead of releasing her, he gripped the back of her head, holding her in place.

His tongue caressed hers. The movements were slow and gentle, as if he was sampling a fine wine—he wanted to take his time, savor the moment, and make it last. At least, that's what she wanted, and she could only hope he felt the same way.

Nicholas's hand slipped to her knee. He slowly moved it to her calf, then back up to the knee. The movement sent a tingle down her legs to the tips of her toes. He moved his hand again, and the sensation increased.

It was the first time a man had ever touched her. Yet she did not fear what would happen next. When Celeste and she were eleven, Nonna Sophie had explained what occurred between a man and woman, so neither girl would have to wait until her wedding night, as she had.

With each stroke, Nicholas's hand moved farther past her knee, until he pushed back the hem of the pajama top. A breeze caressed the juncture between her legs, reminding Georgia of her lack of clothes. She had not thought about it when he walked into the room; her mind had been on the bar. But with his lips on hers and his fingers stroking her leg, she was more than aware of what he would come in contact with if he moved his hand much farther up her thigh.

Georgia knew a respectable woman did not let a man between her thighs before they stood before a preacher. She should remind Nicholas she was not one of the women he bedded; she did not give it up at a drop of a hat to whoever was available at the moment. But she was too curious to stop him. Would his touch increase the throbbing between her legs, or offer her relief?

****

Georgia sighed. The noise effectively reminded Nicholas who he was with. He snatched back his hand and broke from the kiss.

Panting, he stepped out of her reach and brushed his hand over his brow. How the hell did Georgia manage to get him more excited with a kiss than his companion of the previous evening with all her experience and her cache of tricks?

"Who taught you that?" His tone was harsher than he intended; besides being excited, he was angry.

The thought of another man kissing her pissed him off. It did not matter that she wasn't his nor would she ever be. He did not want anyone else with her.

Nicholas was also angry at himself. The kiss was not supposed to excite him. He was supposed to be turned off, so things could go back to the way they were.

Georgia's eyes narrowed. She slid off the windowsill and started toward the door. Nicholas realized he was about to get his wish. Things would go back to the way they were when they were not speaking to each other.

Nicholas rushed after her and grabbed her arm. He could not let her walk away again. She meant too much to him.

"You've got a lot of—"

"I'm sorry."

He knew he had a lot of nerve questioning what she was doing and who she did it with. That was her business and would only become his if she chose to reveal it. Otherwise, for the sake of their friendship, he needed to leave it alone.

The angry creases in Georgia's forehead faded as quickly as they appeared. She nodded her acceptance of his apology. The gesture was not enough.

Though he knew it would pain him in the long run, Nicholas pulled her toward him. When she allowed him to hold her, he knew she forgave him.

Chapter 14

"What are you doing?'

Georgia squeaked as she spun around and peeped over the top of the sofa. She could have sworn Nicholas was sleeping when she looked at him seconds earlier.

He grimaced as she rested her forearms on the back of his makeshift bed. His hair stuck out to the left, right, and in front of him, yet she suspected it would be flat in the back when he sat up. Crust had formed in the corner of his eyes, and the stubble on his face had ceased being a five-o'clock shadow twenty-four hours ago.

His shirt lay across the back of the sofa, next to Georgia's arm. His sleeveless undershirt was hiked up, revealing the fine line of hair between his navel and the waist of his pants. Her eyes continued lower to the generous bulge in the front of his pants. She stared until he reached for the afghan under her arms and tugged it over him.

"Well?" he grumbled. "What were you doing?"

Georgia's cheeks warmed as she returned her attention to his face. It wasn't the first time she'd noticed the bulge when he woke in the morning. After being on the receiving end of one too many pranks by his sister, he had learned to sleep lightly—a habit a fifteen-year-old Georgia had discovered during a sleepover.

On a dare, she had snuck into Nicholas's bedroom

with a washcloth she had placed in the refrigerator the previous night. As she prepared to drop the cold cloth on his face, he reached up, grabbed her wrists, and pulled her onto the bed. Once he had her pinned down, he dropped the cloth on her face.

Squealing, Georgia had squirmed under him until he hissed. She stopped moving as he froze, his morning wood pressed against her leg. A second passed before his face turned red. He rolled off her and ordered her out the room as he tried to cover his lower regions with the bed sheet.

His tone had indicated dawdling was not an option, and Georgia scrambled from beneath him and out of the room. She stopped in the hall to consider what had happened.

The experience had not repulsed or scared her. Instead, she had been left curious as to what he looked like without his pajama bottoms. She, however, had not found out, as he'd moved into his own place not too long after the incident, stating it was time he was on his own.

"Are you going to stand there with a goofy grin on your face all day?"

Georgia shrugged as she tried to regain her composure.

"Since you're not sure, go find someplace else to stand."

"Fine, I'll go make breakfast."

"Hell, no." He struggled to sit up, obviously sore from sleeping on the sofa. What he went through for her was above and beyond what was considered necessary for a friend.

"Would you like me to rub your back for you?"

Georgia asked, wanting to do something in return for his kindness.

"Don't touch me."

With a speed she did not think possible, Nicholas shot off the sofa and jumped out of her reach.

Georgia cocked an eyebrow. She stood up straight and crossed her arms over her chest. "Why not?" She tried not to laugh at his behavior.

"You touch me, and I won't be liable for what I do next." He wiped his hand across his face. "Go find something to do."

"I told you I was going to make breakfast, and you said 'no.' "

"No offense, but you're not the best cook."

Georgia shrugged her shoulders. No offense taken. She knew she did not have any culinary skills. Her father had passed on what little knowledge he had to her. And he could only ensure they did not end up in the hospital with food poisoning.

She wondered how much better Nicholas thought he could do. She had never seen him step foot in a kitchen, unless he was about to eat.

During her last visit, no one had gone near the room. In the morning, a hungover Celeste had begged them to spare her the agony of having to smell anything stronger than water.

"Go use the bathroom so I can get in there," Nicholas said. "I'll fix breakfast once I'm done."

"I've already used the shower."

He waved his hand toward the hall. "Then go get dressed."

Georgia folded her arms over her chest. "If sleeping on the sofa's going to make you that cranky, next time I'll sleep on it and you take the bed."

"Not happening."

"I could suggest we both—"

"Go," Nicholas ordered.

**\*\*\*\***

He knew he had not been as loud as he intended when Georgia did not scurry out of the room. She huffed before she sauntered away, her hips gently swaying from side to side. He did not know if her movements were intentional or not. Either way, it had the same effect on him.

Nicholas had not thought it was possible to get harder than he had been last night, but the fullness in his underwear alerted him that it was not only possible but downright uncomfortable.

He started down the hall as Georgia stepped into the bedroom and closed the door. What was going on with his body? The pajamas were several sizes too big on her. The top was buttoned to the neck, and she had not bothered to roll up the sleeves, so only her head showed. She had to hold up the front of the pajama pants to avoid tripping over them when she walked. Yet his libido was responding to her as if she were prancing around in skimpy lingerie.

Nicholas ducked into the bathroom and turned on the shower. To his relief, Georgia's underwear was no longer hanging from the rod.

He quickly shed the rest of his clothes and stepped under the refreshing spray. He was more than a bit ripe. The previous night, after hugging Georgia, he'd retreated from the room before he gave in to the temptation to kiss her again. When he reached the living room, he realized he had forgotten—for the second time—to grab a change of clothes. Since he was spending another night in his clothes, he had not seen the purpose of showering then.

Before he could wash away the grime, he needed relief. Closing his eyes, he tried to conjure up the image of a voluptuous Alice, stretched out on her bed, wearing nothing but a leer. Yet no matter how hard he concentrated, the only woman who came to mind was Georgia.

The memory of her bare legs and the softness of her thighs beneath his fingertips haunted him. He wondered…if he had not stopped, would she have allowed him to go further? If so, how much further?

After a minute, Nicholas gave up trying to force the images in his mind. Instead, he took care of his needs while thinking of the woman he could not have. He reasoned that as long as he kept his hands—and all other body parts—off her, there was no harm in dreaming.

Once he found the release he had sought, he slumped against the wall. Something told him it would not be enough. Like an addict, he was going to need more and more to get him through the day.

When he finally stepped out of the shower, he realized he once again had failed to get a change of clothes. Sighing, he wrapped a towel around his waist and cracked open the bathroom door.

The aroma of coffee drifted down the hall. Pots clanged on the stove.

"I told you I was going to cook."

"I just put on the coffee," Georgia called back. "I've never had any complaints about that."

"Just don't touch anything else." He opened the

door wider. "And don't come out of the kitchen."

He wasn't surprised when the brat's head popped out of the kitchen. Her gaze slowly moved from his damp hair and down his bare chest and finally stopped at the towel. "Then what do you want me to do?" With a lecherous grin, she leered at him as if she was waiting for the towel to fall.

He adjusted his grip on the terrycloth covering to prevent her from getting her wish. "Stay there and drink your coffee." He waved her back with his free hand.

After a heartbeat, she shrugged her shoulders, then retreated into the kitchen. He waited until he heard her rummaging through a cabinet before he stepped into the hall. He rushed to the bedroom and closed the door.

The bed was made and the pajamas she had worn were neatly folded on the edge. Despite the torture her presence caused him, he would always leave the welcome mat out for her. Anyone willing to straighten up behind herself would never be turned away by him.

Nicholas threw on a T-shirt and jeans, then headed for the kitchen before Georgia disobeyed his order not to touch anything. To his relief, she sat in the chair near the window, scanning through a newspaper. The table was set, the necessary pots were on the stove, and all the ingredients he needed were lined up on the counter.

"Where'd you get that?" He pointed to the newspaper.

"The newsstand," she replied as she neatly folded the rag. "I went out while you were in the shower."

"You must've run. I didn't know you were gone."

"Or you could've been in the shower that long. Sheesh, I take less time in the bathroom...even when I wash my hair and shave my legs." She dropped the paper next to her plate. "What were you doing in there?"

"None of your business." He silently groaned as the image of her legs popped into his mind.

She sucked her teeth. "Drink your coffee." She pointed to the mug in front of his plate. "Maybe it'll help your disposition."

Spending the next three hours locked in the bedroom with her was the only thing that would help him. However, as that was not an option, he picked up the mug and gulped down his coffee.

The liquid burned his throat and brought tears to his eyes. It also did a wonderful job of taking his mind away from an activity he could not engage in.

He slammed the mug onto the counter. Georgia shook her head as she raised her own mug and took a normal sip. He was certain she was one step away from calling someone to lock him up. Who knew, maybe what his grandmother told him when he was growing up was true…masturbation caused insanity.

Nicholas poured another cup of coffee. Following Georgia's example, he took a normal sip before setting the mug aside. As he reached for the butter, he blocked out everything around him. Whenever he stepped into the kitchen, he focused on the task at hand. His grandmother had taught him that a meal will come out half-assed if he only gave it half his attention. It was a lesson he took to heart, and he was well rewarded whenever he sat at his two-chair table.

Fifteen minutes later, Georgia's mouth dropped open when he turned from the stove with the pan in his hand and spooned cheese eggs onto their plates. After placing the pan in the sink, he added a platter of toast and pancetta to the center of the table.

"Help yourself."

Georgia spooned a forkful of eggs into her mouth. Her eyes widened as she tasted the food, and he swore she groaned as she swallowed.

"Where'd you learn how to cook like this?" she asked as she reached for a slice of toast.

"Nonna."

"But your father's always complaining that you and Celeste don't know your way around the kitchen."

Nicholas slid into the chair across from her. "Celeste doesn't, but I do."

"Why didn't you tell him?"

"'Cause he'd insist I work at the club." He swept half the pancetta off the platter onto his plate and grabbed four slices of toast.

"And what's wrong with that?"

"That was his dream. Not mine."

She nodded in understanding as she grabbed two slices of toast.

Nicholas held out his hand, and she passed him the newspaper. He opened to the first page. His hand froze with the forkful of eggs halfway to his mouth as his gaze landed on an article in the lower right-hand corner.

"What's wrong?" Georgia asked, her voice filled with concern.

"The police found a body in a dumpster three blocks from your father's bar."

"Oh, that." The concern switched to indifference.

Nicholas looked up from the picture of the severely beaten man. Carl...Earl...whatever the hood's name was...hung out on the same corner where they found his body. On more than one occasion Nicholas had witnessed a transaction between him and someone who obviously needed his next fix.

Nicholas had taken an instant dislike to the young man because of his chosen profession. He came to loathe the dealer after the man called Georgia out of her name due to her association with the Santianos.

During one confrontation, Nicholas had slammed on the brake and shifted his car into park in the middle of the street before he jumped out and went after the other man. He had been prepared to make him swallow every tooth in his mouth, but Georgia ran to his side and begged him not to resort to violence. He allowed her to pull him back to the car. As he drove away, he fumed about her passive beliefs.

Yet this morning she sat across from Nicholas, eating as if nothing was amiss. Her eyes showed no emotion for the young man or the horrific beating he had sustained.

Nicholas remembered the interaction between Georgia and his father the previous afternoon in the hospital room. Showing off was the quickest way to get caught when taking matters into his own hands. Though witnesses would spread the word of the consequences of messing with family, they would also tattle when confronted by the authorities. Therefore, whenever there was a confrontation it was best to limit the number of people involved and never discuss what transpired.

It was for that reason he knew neither his father nor Georgia would talk about the young man's death. However, he had no need for them to confirm his suspicions. He knew his father had a hand in the dealer's demise and that not only was Georgia aware of the role he'd played but she approved.

Nicholas closed the paper and dropped it into the garbage behind him. He was disgusted that someone could be so evil that his death would elicit no emotions from the most peace-loving person he knew.

Once they finished breakfast, Georgia insisted on doing the dishes. The chore did not take long, since Nicholas always cleaned as he prepared food, to minimize the mess he had to work around. Also, if there was one thing he did not enjoy, it was tackling a sink full of dishes on a full stomach, when all he wanted to do was lounge around in front of the television.

Georgia strolled into the bedroom as he was brushing his hair. He watched her reflection in the mirror. Her face was brighter than it had been the previous day, and her eyes were more alert. She stood tall, with her shoulders back, capable of taking on the world.

"You ready?"

She nodded.

Nicholas tossed the brush on the dresser. He took her hand and gave it a reassuring squeeze before leading her out of the apartment.

****

Georgia's shoulders slumped. She did not know where to begin.

The damage to the bar was worse than what she remembered. The majority of the furniture appeared beyond repair. And she did not think there was a bottle of liquor left intact.

Nicholas patted her shoulder. She was grateful for his presence. Without him, she did not think she would be able to stand there. Yes, the previous night she had

166

talked about cleaning up and opening back up, but talk was cheap. Action was what mattered most, and if she had been by herself, she was certain she would have followed her instinct to curl up in the middle of the room and cry.

"Go upstairs and change. I'll get everything we'll need."

Georgia headed upstairs. She first called Joey to apologize for not showing up for work the previous day. It did not come as a surprise that he had already heard about the attack on her father. The Santianos were quick to pass on news regarding family and friends.

After her employer gave her his best wishes, she changed into a pair of denim capris and one of her father's old shirts. Though her father insisted ladies did not wear pants, she owned two pairs. She preferred them over dresses when she helped with the quarterly cleaning and maintenance of the bar.

When she returned to the bar, Elvis Presley's "That's All Right" drifted from an old radio her father had stored in the back room after he purchased the newer model. Leave it to Nicholas to turn to music her father called noise.

A mop and broom leaned against one end of the bar. Several rags lay on top. The salvageable bottles of liquor were lined up on the other end.

Nicholas stood behind the bar, pouring a shot of whiskey.

"You know Daddy wouldn't like you drinking his liquor."

Nicholas reached into his back pocket and pulled out his wallet. He dropped a twenty on the bar and shoved the billfold back into place.

"That's too much."

"He'll owe me a couple." He raised the glass to her, then downed the liquor.

Shaking her head, she walked behind the bar to ring up the sale. She pressed a button and the register dinged and the drawer slid open.

Georgia gasped.

"What's up?"

Nicholas glanced over her shoulder at the full drawer. She was sure that if she counted the money there would be more than her father usually took in on a Thursday night.

"Your father shouldn't have."

"What makes you think Pops is behind this?"

Georgia glanced back. Like father, like son. Reveal nothing, play innocent, but be there for a friend in a time of need.

Before she could reply, the bell over the door tinkled. Georgia glanced past Nicholas at the young man entering. His lips were turned down in a frown, worry lines marred his olive complexion, and tears hovered at the brim of his downcast eyes.

"I'm sorry, Georgia." His voice cracked.

She rushed from behind the bar to the young man who was two years her junior. "It's all right, Ray," she said, embracing him.

She felt his head shake against hers. "No, it's my fault."

Georgia pulled back and stared into his hazel eyes. "Why's that?"

"I shouldn't have left him."

"You were here?"

He nodded. "I came in early on Thursday and was sweeping when Earl walked in with his shadows. Your father said he needed me to run an errand and once I was finished, I was to call it a night. Something told me to stay, but he insisted."

"I'm glad you listened to him. If not, you'd be lying in a hospital bed next to him."

"Still—"

"Stop beating yourself up. You know there's no way he'd have let you stay, even if he had to toss you out of here himself."

The stubborn set in his jaw said Raymond would continue to blame himself. "What are you going to do?" He glanced around the room.

"Exactly what Daddy would've done. I'm going to clean this place and open up."

"You'll need help." He reached for the broom and nodded toward Nicholas. "I haven't seen you in a while."

"Been busy," Nicholas replied. He looked at Georgia before adding, "But I've put things into perspective."

The two men stared at each other. Though they did not say a word, she felt like they had made plans about her life without consulting her.

Georgia opened her mouth to give both men a piece of her mind. A quick glance at the task ahead of her forced her mouth shut; she swallowed her complaint. Better to have them stick around and help while thinking they had some say in her life than to have them walk out and force her to deal with the mess on her own. With a huff, she righted the chair next to her and inspected the damage.

**\*\*\*\***

"Here's another one."

Georgia set the chair on top of a table to the right of the door, where they were placing the furniture in need of repairs. The stack to the left was the furniture that was beyond repair and slated for the junkyard. Unfortunately, the pile on the left was larger than the one on the right, and together they were far more than the usable stack in the back.

The damage had been more extensive than Nicholas had originally anticipated. With only a half dozen chairs sturdy enough to hold a body and two tables undamaged, there was next to no place other than the bar for people to sit while they enjoyed their drinks. If it wouldn't have taken the paperwork so long to get through, he would have suggested they apply for a cabaret license and turn the center of the room into a dance floor.

Georgia's shoulders drooped again. Nicholas knew she was beginning to feel overwhelmed at the task ahead of her. Not only did she have to take care of the bar, but her father would need care, too, once he was released from the hospital.

Feeling the need to lighten the mood, Nicholas turned up the volume on the radio as the first beats of Eddie Cochran's "C'mon Everybody" played. He strutted back to Georgia, took her hands, and led her toward the center of the room.

"What are you doing?"

"Granted, I'm not an expert, but I think most people would call this dancing." He slipped one hand around her waist and bopped in time to the music.

"Nick, be serious. My father doesn't have a cabaret

license."

"It's only needed if there are three or more people dancing. As long as Ray doesn't join in, we're fine."

"You don't have to worry about me," Raymond called from behind the bar, where he was sweeping up broken glass. "This ain't my kind of music."

"See, it's all right. Relax and enjoy yourself."

He felt her relax in his arms. Her lips turned up in a smile. He spun her away from him and her melodic laughter blended with the music. But when he pulled her back, her body began to shake and her laughter turned to sobs.

Nicholas stopped moving. "Sshh, it's all right." He held Georgia to his chest and rubbed her back.

"No, it's not." She shook her head. "I'm a horrible daughter."

"No, you're not."

"Yes, I am. I'm over here dancing and laughing while my father's in the hospital."

"There's nothing wrong with enjoying yourself. You know your father would not want you moping around."

"How would you know what he wants? It's not like you've ever sat down and talked to him. He doesn't even like you."

"Whatever you say. You can lash out at me all you want."

"Stop being nice to me."

"Sure, anything you say," Nicholas agreed without releasing her.

He kissed the top of her head as he gently rocked her. When her sobs finally calmed to a whimper, he pulled back and brushed the tears from her cheeks. "Do you feel better?"

Georgia shook her head.

"Do you want to cry some more?"

She shook her head again.

"Do you want me to just hold you?"

She nodded.

He pushed her back to his chest as the bell over the door tinkled.

"What the hell's goin' on?"

Georgia tensed and tried to pull back. Nicholas maintained his grip on her as he glanced over her head at her friend.

"We're cleaning. Whaddaya think we're doing?"

"Funny, it looks more like yah feelin' her up."

Nicholas cocked an eyebrow. Georgia's so-called perfect man abandoned her at the first chance he got and then had the nerve to fume over her finding comfort elsewhere.

"Nicholas…"

Sighing at Georgia's use of his first name instead of the abbreviation, he reluctantly released her but stayed near her side. Raymond lowered the volume on the radio.

"Where've you been?" her friend shouted despite the decrease in background noise.

"That's none of your business."

Nicholas smiled. He was proud she refused to let the other man intimidate her.

"It is when we had a date."

"Our plans weren't definite. I told you I'd think about it." Georgia shook her head. "Besides, you didn't expect me to go out last night, with my father in the hospital, did you?"

"It's not like you were sittin' at home waitin' for news."

"I don't have to explain myself to you." She placed one hand on her hip and pointed to the door with the other. "William, go home until you want to be reasonable."

The man's mouth dropped open. He looked like he was not used to having anyone…especially a woman…dismiss him. He took a step and reached out for her. He missed his target as Nicholas stepped between the two.

"I think the lady asked you to leave."

The other man grimaced as he glanced from Georgia to him and then back. After a second, he held up his hands and backed away. "You're right. Things are getting a bit tense around here…you know…with your father not around. I'll come back later and we can talk."

Georgia nodded. Nicholas did not approve, yet he decided not to add to her aggravation by voicing his opinion. He simply stood there until the other man walked out and the door closed behind him.

"I don't like him." Raymond voiced what Nicholas had been thinking.

Georgia looked at the young man. "That's unfair. You don't know him."

"I've a feeling about him."

Georgia pursed her lips together as if she was trying to hold back an argument. She was unable to tell him a "feeling" held no merit. Not after she claimed she'd had one about Gianni.

Nicholas realized he had yet to bring up the reason they had not talked for several weeks. But that was another topic for another time.

The telephone rang, breaking the tension. Raymond picked up the handset and listened. A smile grew on his face. After a second, he told the other party to hold on. He then held out the handset and announced, "Your father's awake."

Chapter 15

"You look worse than what the cat drug in," her father mumbled as she rushed into the room.

Georgia shook her head. She had known he'd have something to say about her outfit, but she had been too eager to see him to change from her pants into a skirt.

"What I look like doesn't matter." She leaned over the side of the bed and placed a kiss on his forehead. "How do you feel?"

"Like somethin' the cat drug in."

She smiled as she walked to the empty chair on the other side of the bed. At least he was maintaining his sense of humor.

"The doctor explained all your injuries and said you're going to be here for least a week."

"Yeah, whatever. It ain't like he got a bar to tend to."

"Don't worry about the bar. Nick and I spent the morning cleaning and taking inventory of what's needed. I'll place the orders on Monday."

Her father turned his head and glared at Nicholas, who leaned against the doorjamb. A smile spread across his lips as if the older man's actions amused him.

"You know where I keep the emergency fund. Do what you can with it."

"It won't be necessary. There was plenty in the drawer to cover the expenses," Georgia replied, wondering if the doctor should reexamine her father's head. She never expected he'd agree to her helping out with the bar.

He closed his eyes and shook his head. His lips moved, yet she could not make out what he was mumbling. After a minute he frowned at her, and she shook her head.

"I didn't ask anyone for the money."

"I know you didn't, girl. Though you're still to blame."

"Why's that?"

"'Cause of your kindness. That man would've never filled up that drawer if you weren't a good girl."

"Then if anyone's to take the blame, you should. You're the one who taught me right."

"I concede." Her father chuckled. "So what else have you've been up to?"

"Nothing else, Daddy. I've just been worrying about you."

She conveniently left out where she had been worrying. She did not want to be responsible for the coronary he'd have if she told him she'd stayed at Nicholas's apartment.

"By the way, William sends his best."

"Now, he's the type of man you should be hangin' wit'."

Her father was impossible. He couldn't let up with his matchmaking for a second. She suspected he would actually consider the brief make-out session in the car a positive sign.

Unfortunately for William, the kiss had been another strike against him. It had been a disappointment, and she had been eager to get away from him. She, however, had enjoyed every moment with Nicholas and regretted his pulling away. In fact, she was certain she would have allowed him to continue if he had not stopped.

"Are you all right, girl?"

Georgia snapped out of her thoughts. "Yes, why?" She forced a weak grin on her lips.

"You had this funny look on your face."

Her cheeks warmed. "It's nothing, Daddy," she said as she raised her eyes to peep at Nicholas.

He didn't notice her look. He had been focusing on something in the hall and now stepped out of the room. A second later, he ushered in Celeste.

"I hope I'm not bothering you."

"You know you're always welcome." Georgia's father spoke for the entire room.

Too excited to speak, Georgia jumped out of her chair. By the time she reached the door, Nicholas had grabbed the bouquet of flowers from his sister's hand and slid her coat off her other arm.

When they were younger, Georgia and Celeste would squeal and embrace each time they met as if they not seen each other days. This time, it had been weeks, not hours, since the women last spoke. While they did not emit high-pitched noises that would have nurses running to the room to investigate, they hugged one another with just as much fervor.

After a minute-long embrace, the women stepped back. Through the tears falling from their eyes, they sized each other up. Though Celeste's hair was pulled back in a single braid, it lacked luster. She had circles under her eyes and had lost enough weight that her clothes hung off her small frame.

Georgia's eyes dropped to the bruise peeping from her friend's short sleeve. She reached up and touched the arm. Celeste jerked back and grimaced, but her features quickly straightened. With a small laugh, Celeste wiped the tears from her cheeks with the back of her hand.

"It's nothing," her friend explained before anyone had a chance to ask questions. "I walked into a wall the other night. You know how clumsy I am."

Georgia shook her head as she wiped her own face. She didn't remember her friend being clumsy. The only time she could recall Celeste ever walking into anything was the night of their prom, and the woman had been smashed at the time.

"I was sorry to hear what happened, Mr. Collins." Celeste reached for the flowers Nicholas had rescued. "I got you these. I wasn't sure if you'd like them."

He lifted his left hand, and she placed the bouquet in the crook of his arm.

"They're beautiful. Come, sit down."

Nicholas slipped out of the room as Celeste took the chair Georgia had vacated.

"I've missed havin' you around the apartment. It's so quiet without the two of you gigglin' at all hours of the night."

"You couldn't have heard us, Mr. Collins."

He snorted. "Y'all used to make such a racket the deaf man in the next block complained y'all kept him up."

Nicholas returned with another chair and a vase. He placed the second chair next to his sister.

"Thank you," Georgia said as she slid into the empty seat.

Nicholas winked at her before he disappeared into the bathroom. A second later, Georgia heard the sound of water splashing against glass.

"So how's married life treatin' you?" her father asked.

Celeste flinched. It had been a slight gesture, one Georgia would have missed had she not been staring directly at her friend.

"It's fine." Celeste's voice was unnaturally high, as if she was trying to force herself to sound cheerful. "I never realized how much work goes into taking care of a house, but Gio's so patient with me. He's so understanding when I do things wrong."

Georgia glanced at her father, who rolled his eyes. He also wasn't buying the load of bull Celeste was dishing out. The young woman, however, did not appear to notice the silent exchange as she continued to praise the virtues of a man Georgia suspected was no more honorable than the serpent was with Eve.

Nicholas walked back into the room. He passed the filled vase to Georgia, who held it out to Celeste. Her friend took the vase and placed it on the nightstand next to her. The movement caused her sleeve to rise. The bruise was wider than Georgia's fist. It was more the size of a man's fist. If she had to guess, she'd say the fist belonged to Gianni.

"Celeste, I haven't eaten anything since breakfast. Do you mind walking to the cafeteria with me?"

"Of course not. It's…it's just…" Celeste's cheeks reddened.

"It's just what?"

"I don't have any money. I spent it all on the bus and the flowers."

179

The confession made Georgia more suspicious. Celeste used to walk around with enough cash in her purse to go shopping at Bergdorf Goodman, have lunch at the Waldorf Astoria, and then pay a driver to take her from Manhattan to Brooklyn. Now she was claiming broke after spending fifteen cents for a bus ride and a dollar fifty for a small bouquet of daisies.

"No problem." Georgia smiled up at Nicholas.

Shaking his head, he pulled out his wallet. "Will a fiver do?"

"That's more than enough." She stood, walked over to him, and took the five-dollar bill from him, then waved toward the door. "Come on."

Celeste slowly rose from her chair and shuffled across the room. They headed down the hall to the elevator in silence. Neither spoke until they were seated at a table in the corner.

"What's going on, Celeste?"

Her friend shrugged her shoulders. She ripped the wrapper off her chicken sandwich and tore into her food as if she had not eaten in days. Georgia lost her appetite, watching. She silently placed her sandwich on Celeste's tray.

"Nothing's going on," Celeste replied after she swallowed the bite she'd been chewing.

"Come on, it's me you're talking to. I know you better than anyone else does."

Celeste dropped her gaze to her tray as she shoved more food into her mouth.

"Is Gianni hitting you?"

Her friend squared her shoulders. She vehemently shook her head. Yet Georgia noticed the mixture of fear and sorrow in her friend's eyes.

"How could you ask me something like that?"

"The bruise on your arm."

"I told you, I walked into a wall."

"I'd believe that if you weren't the most coordinated person I know."

Celeste's shoulders slumped.

"If he's hurting you, you need to tell someone."

"Gianni would never hurt anyone. He's the kindest, most gentle man—"

"And he's patient and understanding…" Georgia ticked off the virtues on her fingers as she repeated the list her friend had recited while they were upstairs.

"Stop making fun of me."

Georgia dropped her hands. The last thing she wanted to do was antagonize Celeste; however she could not back down until she got the truth.

She reached across the table and held her friend's hand. "Do you remember what your father used to tell us?"

Though Celeste nodded, Georgia repeated the lecture the man gave them when they were old enough to date. "We're princesses in our fathers' eyes and princesses deserve princes. A prince would go out of his way to make a princess happy. He'd never do anything to make her cry, and he'd sooner chop off his own hands than lay them on her in anger."

"I remember," Celeste whispered.

"So, if anything is going on—"

"Why should you care?" Celeste's voice rose, attracting the attention of the diners at the next table. "You couldn't even bother showing up for my party."

Georgia shook her head. "I did show up, but I was told it was a private party."

"That's impossible. I told them to let you in the moment you arrived."

She opened her mouth, then quickly snapped it shut. They could go back and forth all day in a he-said-she-said debate and never resolve the problem. It wasn't what Georgia wanted. She preferred them to put everything behind them and be friends again.

"I don't want to argue anymore."

Celeste dropped her head, but not before Georgia saw her unshed tears.

****

Neither woman looked like the reunion had been a joyous one. Celeste appeared ready to burst into tears any second. Georgia was tense and seemed like she would snap at the first person who looked at her wrong.

"Is everything all right?" Nicholas asked.

"Everything's fine," Celeste mumbled as she walked around to the other side of the bed. She leaned over the bed and gave Mr. Collins a kiss. "I hope you feel better soon."

"You're leavin'?"

"I have to get dinner ready. Gianni likes to eat before he goes to the club."

"In that case, I'm glad you stopped by."

"Do you mind giving Celeste a ride home?" Georgia asked Nicholas.

"Let me know when you're ready," he replied.

Georgia stepped up to the bed. "Daddy—"

"Go do what you need to do."

"Thank you." She placed a kiss on his cheek. "Behave yourself and don't give the doctors a hard time."

He snorted. "She thinks she's grown enough to tell

me what to do."

"Till you're out of that bed, yes, I am."

Both women walked away from the bed. Nicholas gave the older man a curt nod before following them out of the room.

"Thanks for the ride," Celeste said as they waited for the elevator. "I wasn't sure how I was going to get home in time to get dinner on. I hope you'll excuse me for not inviting you over, but I'm still trying to learn my way around the kitchen."

"Is everything all right…you know, moneywise?" Nicholas asked.

His sister chuckled. "Of course, why wouldn't it be? Gianni said the club's doing fine."

Yes, business was fine, if the club was supposed to cater to a seedy crowd. Their father had envisioned a more upscale venue, and though Nicholas had not been interested in taking over the business, he did not want to see his father's dream dissolve.

"When was the last time you were at the club?"

"My birthday. Gianni prefers me to take care of the house. He handles the club."

"Since you haven't started dinner, why don't we stop by the club? We'll head back to my place. You can call Gianni from there and tell him to meet us there."

"I'm not dressed for going out," Georgia replied.

"I think I saw a blue dress in the back of my closet."

"I'm missing a blue dress."

Celeste gave her a weak smile. "I thought the color looked good on me."

"So, whaddaya think?" Nicholas asked.

"I think I need to go through your closet." Georgia

sighed as she stepped off the elevator and marched toward the door.

Chapter 16

Georgia stopped short as she stepped into the dining room at Gracie's. She had thought her plain blue dress would be too casual. Yet a quick scan of the crowd told her she was overdressed.

The majority of the women wore dresses more suited for standing on the street corner, while the men reminded her of guys one could not pay a woman to be with.

The once pristine establishment looked like the cleaning crew had quit. The tables were bare and the linen napkins had been replaced by dispensers that stored paper products. She took sparse breaths so as not to gag on the stench of cheap perfume, watered-down liquor, and tobacco smoke.

Gianni stood in front of the band, conversing with two large men who gave Georgia the chills. Both looked dangerous, the type she would not want to bump into on a well-lit street, and she suspected they were packing. A woman wearing a tight, low-cut dress and gaudy jewelry stood, in Georgia's opinion, much too close to Gianni. He apparently forgot he was a married man and reached around and groped the woman's derriere.

Georgia glanced at Celeste. The other woman's face turned red, yet Georgia suspected her friend would not say anything to her husband about his habit of groping other women.

After a second, one of the men glanced in their direction. His eyes locked on Georgia. Her skin crawled as he leered at her. It felt like he was not only undressing her with his eyes, but imagining what he would do to her once she was rid of all her clothes.

Without a word Nicholas's hand closed around hers and he pulled her behind him. The man's leer turned to a scowl. He silently challenged Nicholas. When her companion did not back down, the other man leaned in and whispered to Gianni.

The man who had vowed to forsake all others slowly glanced in their direction. He then turned back to the men, his hand moving only an inch up from his companion's rear. Once the goons walked off, Gianni's arm snaked around the woman's waist. He leaned over and whispered in the hussy's ear. She stared at Nicholas, her lips twisted in a mocking grin.

Nicholas squeezed Georgia's hand as if trying to get the strength to keep from flying across the room and laying into someone. However, she did not think he would get what he needed from her. She wanted to step forward and wipe the grin from the woman's face before laying into Gianni.

How could they carry on in front of Celeste like she didn't matter? Her friend was a good person and did not deserve to be treated with such disrespect. She should be with a man who not only had enough class not to flaunt his women in front of his wife but didn't have other women to begin with.

Before Georgia could snatch her hand from Nicholas's and start across the room, the other woman pecked Gianni on the cheek and sashayed over to the bar.

"What are you doing here?" Gianni asked as he stepped around the tables to get to them.

Celeste squirmed when his gaze fell on her. After a second, he turned his attention to Georgia. She, however, did not cower at the flash of the disdain in his eyes.

"We were at the hospital, visiting Georgia's father." Nicholas glanced from Georgia to Gianni. "I figured we could have dinner here tonight. Maybe get to know one another."

Gianni's face went blank when he looked at his friend. "Celeste was with you?"

"I went to the hospital to visit Mr. Collins," Celeste said. "I took him flowers."

Georgia noticed the tick in the man's chin. Instead of replying, he waved them to a table in the shadows.

As they walked through the room, she realized she was the only person of color not waiting tables. Though the establishment had been an upscale Italian eatery, when Mr. Santiano ran the club it was integrated; it had not been unusual to see coloreds dining as well as whites.

Once they were seated, Gianni raised his arm and snapped his fingers. Across the room, the bartender reached under the bar and retrieved a bottle. A waiter grabbed the drink as another picked up four glasses. Halfway across the room, the two men were joined by a third carrying menus.

By the time they reached the table, the waiters had filed into a single line. The first waiter placed a glass in front of each diner. He stepped to the side and the next waiter poured the drinks. Once he was finished, the last waiter stepped forward and passed out the menus.

As he handed Georgia her menu, his eyes locked with hers. She saw his disapproval and wondered if he considered her a traitor for dining at the establishment.

"I've made a couple of changes," Gianni announced as they opened their menus.

"A couple of changes" was an understatement. Patrons had once been able to enjoy filet mignon, oysters, and a variety of Italian dishes prepared from the recipes passed down from one generation of Santianos to the next. The menu they stared at had the same fare offered in the hospital cafeteria.

"Whaddaya think?"

"Quite a lot of changes you've made," Nicholas stated. "It's not exactly what Pops was going for when he opened this place."

"I'm taking the place in another direction."

"I think I'll just have a slice of toast and tea," Celeste announced. She closed her menu and laid it on the table.

"Live it up a little." Gianni wiped at his nose with the back of his hand. "I promise you the cooking here's better than yours."

Celeste flinched.

"Cooking's not easy," Georgia said.

"It's all right. I know I'm not the best cook."

Georgia shook her head. She would stand up for her friend, even if the woman refused to do it for herself.

"It's not all right. No one's born knowing how to cook. It takes time and practice."

"She'd get better if she wasn't so busy running around town, socializing." Gianni sneered at her.

"Celeste needs to remember she's a married woman."

How dare he talk about someone remembering she's married? From what they'd witnessed when they arrived, he was the one who needed the reminder.

Before Georgia could voice her opinion, Celeste reached across the table and touched her hand. With her eyes, the other woman silently pleaded for her not to make an issue of the statement. Though it bothered her to keep quiet, Georgia decided to drop the subject for her friend's sake.

Having once again lost her appetite, Georgia closed her menu and placed it on top of Celeste's.

"I'll also have a slice of toast," she said.

Once Nicholas made his selection, Gianni placed their orders. The men then reminisced about the antics they'd pulled when they were younger, while the women sat quietly, each lost in her own world.

****

Celeste's head dropped forward until her chin touched her collarbone. It then snapped back so hard Nicholas's neck hurt watching her. He glanced at his watch. It was eight o'clock, much too early for her to be dozing off.

Ignoring his wife, Gianni started to tell a story that involved him and another woman in an alley across the street from his Uncle Joey's diner. Nicholas remembered the incident and felt the story was inappropriate for the company they were with. As he opened his mouth to change the subject, Georgia reached across the table and tapped Celeste's arm.

"Are you okay?" she asked.

Gianni stopped midsentence and glared at his wife. Celeste's eyes popped open. She glanced around the table and her face turned red.

"I'm sorry. I didn't mean to nod off."

"Lounging around the house has made you lazy," Gianni commented. He lit a cigarette and blew the smoke in her direction.

Celeste coughed and waved at the air in front of her. "Could you put that out, please? I'm not feeling well."

"Then go home, where you belong."

"I'm not feeling too well myself." Georgia pushed back from the table, scraping her chair on the floor.

That made three of them. Since they walked into the club, two hours earlier, Nicholas had not felt the same peace he used to experience when he visited Gracie's. Instead he felt tense, his stomach turned and his head throbbed.

"Maybe we should call it an evening." He stood. "I'll drive you home."

"I'll take the bus," Georgia replied.

He shook his head. Though it was not late, there was no way he was going to let Georgia or Celeste take the bus.

"What's the big deal?" Gianni leaned back in his chair. "The dames can take the bus home. Sit. Have a drink."

Nicholas wondered what his friend had to drink before they arrived. His behavior had been progressively crasser during the evening. Figuring he should take Gianni up on his offer and stick around to talk to the other man, Nicholas reached in his pocket and pulled out his keys.

"Take the car," he said, passing the keys to Georgia. "I'll get a ride."

She hesitated before she grabbed the keys. For a second he feared she was going to toss them in his face and insist on taking the bus. But after a quick glance at Celeste, she walked off without acknowledging either man.

"Remember the time we banged that dame underneath the boardwalk?" Gianni asked, once the ladies were gone.

Nicholas dropped back in his chair. "What's gotten into you?"

"Whaddaya mean?"

"Your wife walked out of here, she didn't look good, and you're sitting there talk about screwing another woman."

"What's the big deal? It's not like I'm talking about the woman I banged last night."

For his friend's sake, Nicholas assumed the man was joking. If he even suspected otherwise, he would be obligated to make sure Gianni was unable to have sex with anyone, including his wife, ever again.

Gianni wiped at his nose and sniffed.

"What's up with your nose?"

"Nothing," Gianni insisted before he wiped his nose again. "Probably have a cold."

"Maybe you should've gone home with your wife. You could've taken care of each other."

"I got a business to run. You think keeping a roof over her head is easy?"

"I'm sure it's not." Nicholas leaned forward. "So tell me. You're not having problems, are you?"

"Why d'you ask?"

"You seemed a bit harsh with Celeste."

"She knows I didn't mean anything by it."

191

"Even so, you might wanna lay off."

"Yeah, whatever." Gianni refilled their wine glasses. "How's the business?"

Nicholas sat back and shrugged. Though the money was coming in, he was getting a little tired of things. Especially looking for places to set up shop and looking over his shoulder all the time, wondering if the next person he took a bet from would be the one to slap the cuffs on him.

"We should work together," Gianni muttered.

Nicholas glanced around the restaurant. Though he'd never wanted the place, he wouldn't mind restoring the business to something he'd be proud to have his mother's name on.

"Doing what?" He lifted his glass to his lips.

"I was thinking of setting up a couple of tables downstairs…you know, bring a little more action to this joint."

Nicholas spit out the wine he was about to swallow. What the hell was Gianni thinking? He knew anyone married to Celeste had to be straight.

"Have you lost your mind?"

"I know what your old man said, but he's being damn hypocritical. He's not Mr. Model Citizen."

Nicholas would not argue with the truth.

"He needs to think about his little girl," Gianni continued. "What I'm proposing is the difference between a hole in the wall in the slums and a brownstone on Quality Row."

"I'm sure you haven't reached that point."

"I'm always seeing folks from darktown wandering in our neighborhood. The moment I can afford it, I'm packing my bags and getting away from them."

Though they had not stayed in touch, Nicholas knew the newlyweds had moved into a house in Williamsburg, not far from where Georgia lived. He frowned at the less than flattering name some called Bedford Stuyvesant, where the majority of the population was colored.

"All I'm proposing is taking what you already do and turn it into a larger scale operation."

"No." He would not dishonor his mother by running his business in the venue named after her. "If you need help restoring the club to what it used to be, I'll be there. Otherwise, forget it."

"Whatever."

Gianni's dismissive tone conveyed his intention. He was going ahead with his plan, with or without his friend's help.

Nicholas needed to do something before Gianni incurred the wrath of Marco Santiano.

"Listen, why don't I come over for dinner one night, and we can throw around a couple of ideas. Bring the books. Georgia could look them over for you."

"Not a good idea."

"Why not?"

"Celeste isn't ready to entertain."

Nicholas felt like someone had punched him in the gut. As much as he wanted to believe the excuse, he could not pretend his friend was not full of bull. And the more Gianni talked, the less Nicholas wanted to listen.

After another half hour, Nicholas could no longer tolerate the company or the atmosphere. He made a halfhearted excuse, mumbling something about getting up early in the morning, before he dashed out of the club and into a cab that had stopped for another fare. As he barked his address to the driver, he tossed a couple of bills out the window as reparation for stealing the ride. He had not bothered to pay attention to what he gave the waiting couple, though he was certain it was enough to pay for another cab and the time the man planned to spend with the woman.

As the car moved down the street, Nicholas tried to block out everything that had happened after Celeste walked into Mr. Collins's hospital room. As long as he pretended nothing had happened, he did not have to face the fact that there could be something to Georgia's feeling.

"This is good enough," Nicholas said as the taxi stopped across the street from his building. He tossed a couple of bills over the front seat and jumped out. As the taxi drove away, he spotted his car parked in front of his building. Georgia leaned against the passenger side with her back to him.

Once the traffic was clear, Nicholas sprinted across the street and around the car. In the glow from the streetlight, he saw the tears, glistening in her eyes.

"He's hurting her, Nick."

He had expected a lecture about the state of the club and Gianni's jokes at Celeste's expense, but not an accusation of abuse. One of the codes of the Santiano family was that no man should ever take his aggression out on a woman. For the times a man felt an overwhelming need to strike out, he should go to the gym. If that was not possible, he could use the wall for a punching bag. He'd probably walk away with a broken hand, but at least he'd still have his honor.

"Did she tell you that?" He feared her reply. Gianni

hitting Celeste would be considered worse than him cheating on her, and the consequences would be harsher.

"No, but there's that bruise on her arm."

"Celeste said she walked into a wall."

"How can you believe that? Celeste has never walked into anything before." She shook her head. "And how about the things Gianni said to her tonight?"

"He was just kidding around. Maybe he had a bit too much to drink and he took the jokes too far."

Georgia pulled away from him. "I can't believe you're defending him."

"How can I not? This is Gianni we're talking about." Nicholas raked his hand through his hair. He fought the temptation of yanking it out in frustration. "I've known him most of my life. There's no way he'd ever lay a hand on Celeste."

"That's your final answer?" She took a step away from him.

"Georgia, please." He reached out for her.

She shook her head.

"Listen, how about I talk to Gianni. Tell him to cool it with the jokes."

"What about the bruise?"

"If Celeste said she walked into a wall, I'm going to believe her. She's never lied to me before; there's no reason for me to believe she'd start now."

"How can you be so sure?"

Because he had to believe his friend was not as bad as all the signs were pointing him out to be.

Chapter 17

"What are you doing after church?"

Georgia peeped over the top of the newspaper at Nicholas. He knew she did not attend service regularly. Her visit a few weeks back had been the first time she'd stepped foot inside a house of worship in three years.

"What are you doing after mass?" she countered.

Nicholas cocked an eyebrow. He attended church less often than she did. Whenever he was invited to a wedding or baptism, he skipped the ceremony and joined his relatives at the banquet hall for the party.

"Exactly." She raised the newspaper to finish the comic she had been reading before he interrupted her with a silly question.

"You want to go to the movies?"

"I have to—"

"I know you want to finish cleaning the bar, but how about afterwards?"

Georgia lowered the paper again. She stared at Nicholas, searching for signs that he was mocking her. Instead, she saw his concern. The man was determined to look after her.

Sighing, she folded the paper and placed it on the table. "It depends on what you want to see."

"How about a comedy? I know you're not into war or horror movies, and I can't sit through a romance or a drama…not without wanting to smack my head against the wall."

Georgia smiled at the compromise. Unlike William, Nicholas never forced his wishes on her. It was why she sat across from him in his kitchen for the second morning in a row.

After he promised to speak to Gianni about Celeste, Nicholas had invited her to spend the night. Not wanting to be alone in her apartment, she accepted.

"Whaddaya say? I'll throw in dinner."

"Aren't you tired of hanging around me? Wouldn't you prefer to hang out with one of your other women?"

Nicholas shook his head. "At the moment, none of them have what I'm looking for."

"And what's that?"

"Intelligent conversation."

****

The other women were also lacking the ability to offer him comfort with simply their presence. They always needed a verbal, physical, or monetary confirmation about how he felt about them.

It was different with Georgia. She understood what he needed and when. They were able to enjoy each other's company without having to waste a whole bunch of words affirming that the other was great.

It felt right to have her sitting across from him while they each read different sections of the newspaper and ate the breakfast he'd cooked. It was like they had established a comfortable routine years early, though it was only their second morning together.

Nicholas mopped up the last of his syrup with his French toast before rising from the table. He dropped his silverware onto his plate and was prepared to carry it to the sink when Georgia reached out and placed a hand over his.

"I'll take care of the dishes."

His body reacted to her touch as if she was grinding against him while wearing her lace underwear instead of standing two feet from him, dressed in her capris and one of his old red shirts. The electricity coursed through him, awaking his buddy once again.

His reactions to her were getting too intense. It was getting to the point where she was affecting him with simply a glance.

Nicholas nodded as he slid his hand from under hers. "Thanks. I'll take a shower while you do that."

He rushed out of the room before she could remind him that he had already taken a lengthy shower before breakfast.

Nicholas emerged from the bathroom, and Georgia did not comment on his sudden obsession with cleanliness. Instead she finished folding the bedding he had spread over the sofa the previous evening.

"I really wish you'd let me sleep on the sofa," she said.

"You wouldn't be comfortable. It's meant for sitting, not sleeping."

"At least I fit on the sofa. You're either crammed into the small space or hanging off it."

"I'll be fine."

Georgia sighed. "Why do you have to be so stubborn?"

"It's a pleasure meeting you, pot." Nicholas stepped forward and extended his hand. "I'm kettle."

Georgia shoved the bed sheet and pillow into his arms, and he laughed as she headed to the bedroom. He followed and dropped the linen on the chair.

"You're aggravating," she said as she slipped on her shoes.

"But you love me anyway." He wiggled his eyebrows.

She laughed. He preferred the sound over the stress that had been in her tone the past couple of days.

When she had grabbed her handbag and the two other dresses she'd found in his closet, he escorted her out of the building. On the drive to her apartment, she listed everything she needed to do in order to have the bar ready for business the next evening. They then discussed movies until they came up with one they could both sit through.

"You sure you want to get Chinese food?" Nicholas asked as he pulled up in front of the bar. "I'm in the mood for smothered chicken."

"I had that the other night with William."

Nicholas tensed at the mention of the other man. If he could make the potential boyfriend disappear off the face of the planet, all would be right with the world.

"How about some oxtail stew from Miss Yvonne's?"

Georgia smiled. She could never turn down a hearty oxtail stew, and the restaurant also served smothered chicken.

"Fine," Georgia agreed as they stepped into the building and started up the stairs. "Maybe I'll have a slice of black cake for...what the hell?" she mumbled when she reached the landing.

Nicholas stared at the body sprawled on the floor in front of the apartment door.

"Celeste?"

He gasped as his sister raised her head. A patch of

hair had been torn from her head. Her left eye was swollen shut, her nose appeared broken, with dried blood underneath, and her upper lip was split in two places. She grimaced as she clutched her abdomen.

"What happened?" Georgia dropped her dresses and knelt next to her friend.

"I didn't think he'd mind." Celeste's body shook with her sobs.

"Who?" Nicholas knelt on the other side of her.

"Gio." She whispered the name so softly, he barely heard her. "I didn't think he'd mind me visiting Mr. Collins in the hospital."

"He did this 'cause you visited Georgia's father?"

Celeste nodded.

"Has he done this before?"

Celeste dropped her head.

"Has he?" he barked.

His sister flinched.

"Nicholas, stop yelling," Georgia scolded.

He opened his mouth but then snapped it shut. How could she tell him not to yell? She should be lucky he was not cursing up a streak and tearing things apart. The man he had considered a brother had laid hands on his sister. The worst part of it all was that he had refused to listen to the warnings or see the signs.

"Celeste, can you stand?" Georgia asked.

The battered woman shook her head.

"Nicholas, carry her inside."

She stood and unlocked the door as he gathered his sister in his arms. He felt the moisture from her soiled skirt and wondered how long she had waited in the hall for them to return. He stood, and Celeste cried out as Georgia muttered an expletive.

"What's wrong?" he asked as Georgia shook her head.

"She needs a hospital," she said as she kicked her dresses into the apartment. She stepped back, closed the door, and led the way back out to the car.

She opened the passenger door and pushed the seat forward. With a bit of maneuvering, Nicholas laid Celeste in the rear seat and backed out of the car.

As Georgia climbed into the front passenger seat, Nicholas ran around the car and slid behind the steering wheel. With no concern for anyone else on the road, he sped to the hospital, where he parked in the middle of the street. Ignoring the blare of the horns behind him, he jumped out of the car and retrieved Celeste from the back.

Georgia ran ahead and was yelling for help by the time he stepped into the building. A nurse brought a wheelchair, and he placed his sister in it.

"Go move the car," Georgia ordered. She shoved a handkerchief into his hands before she followed her friend.

Unable to move, Nicholas stared down the hall, long after they disappeared. He had had more than his share of fights during his life, but he had never seen anything as vile as Celeste's injuries.

How could Gianni raise his hand to someone as beautiful as Celeste? There was nothing the woman could have done to justify such cruel treatment. She was a kind and gentle soul whose only sin was caring too much for her family and friends.

"Is that your car outside?"

Nicholas ignored the voice as his breakfast jumped in his stomach. Pushing the body aside, he raced down the corridor to the room marked "Utility." He yanked open the door and released the contents of his stomach into the sink.

"What are you, drunk or something?" The voice asked.

"Give me a second," Nicholas gasped as he grasped the sink. He could not appreciate the person's persistence. He needed a moment to process everything that was happening, his role in it, and how he could make things better.

"I need you to move it. Now."

He felt a nudge in his shoulder. Instinctively, he spun around, grabbed the front of the other man's shirt, and stepped forward until he had the person pinned against the wall across from the closet.

"I said, give me a second."

"Nicholas, stop it," Georgia screamed at the same moment his father called out, "Let him go."

Her soft hand covered his. "Nicholas, please. Celeste needs you."

He blinked several times before he could actually focus on the person he was attacking. The blood had drained from the young officer's face.

"Let him go," his father repeated.

Nicholas slowly uncurled his fingers from the shirt of the officer. Once free, the man was pulled to the side and ushered away.

"Pull yourself together," his father ordered. "Then take care of business."

The older man draped an arm around Georgia's shoulders and steered her away from him. Nicholas was tempted to follow and grab her. He wanted…no, he needed…her presence. But, at the same time, he did not deserve it. He had failed Celeste and Georgia and did not deserve comfort until he made things right.

Without a word, Nicholas turned and marched out the door. He climbed into his car and headed to Gracie's. Again, when he arrived at his destination he left his car in the middle of the street.

Another car, one he had not realized had been tailing him, also stopped. Two men climbed out and followed him.

At the front door, the goon stepped toward him. Nicholas did not slow down. Without turning, he knew one of the men pulled back his jacket to let the gun at his side convince the man to let them pass unmolested.

Nicholas stepped into the dining room. Gianni, who was perched on a stool, leaned over the bar. After a second, he raised his head and sniffed before he passed a rolled up bill to Alice. With a smile the woman placed the bill to her nose and leaned forward.

Without a word, Nicholas walked up to the other man, grabbed him by his hair and slammed his head on the bar.

Alice screeched, and Gianni yelled, "What the hell?" as he raised his head. Blood dripped from his nose onto the white powder on the bar.

"You shouldn't have touched her," Nicholas announced as he slammed his former friend's face back onto the bar. He glanced over his shoulder at the wide-eyed woman behind him. "Business is closed."

Alice stepped back until she was clear of the men, then turned and scampered toward the front door.

The shrill of car horns and the grumbles from irate drivers drifted into the building. Nicholas ignored the commotion from the street as he yanked Gianni from the stool. He was going to give the other man just as much of a fighting chance as Celeste had been given…none.

Holding onto the front of Gianni's shirt, he slammed his fist into the other man's face. He did not count the number of blows he administered or keep track of how much time went by. He simply continued until the knuckles on his right hand were red with both his and the other man's blood.

Once his fist was raw, Nicholas switched hands and resumed the punishment. He pummeled what was left of Gianni's face until two sets of hands grabbed him and his former friend slipped from his bloody grip to the floor.

Nicholas struggled to get free of the men who had followed him into the club. Though Gianni was unconscious, he had not suffered enough, but the men refused to release their hold.

"Your job is done," one of the men holding him announced.

Nicholas stopped struggling. As he tried to catch his breath, he glanced around at the four men who had joined them while he took care of Gianni.

"Your father called us. He wants you to return to the hospital. We'll take care of him."

Though his sister's abuser lay in a heap on the floor, Nicholas did not feel satisfaction. He wanted to finish what he started, but his father would never let him do it.

After a minute, the men relaxed their hold enough for him to pull out of their grasp. For once he would respect his father's wishes.

"Take him," he said. "Quick, before I change my

mind."

The two men who had pulled him off each reached for one of Gianni's arms and dragged him out of the club.

After the door closed behind them, Nicholas glanced around the room that had been converted to a dump no respectable person would step foot in. His sister was lying in the hospital. His father's dreams had been destroyed. And it was all because Nicholas had been too stubborn to see the truth.

****

Georgia could not believe her ears. After everything Celeste had gone through, she had the nerve to apologize for all the trouble she caused? If anything, the universe needed to apologize for everything she'd had to deal with…starting with the mark she had been born with.

The universe should then beg her forgiveness for taking away the mother who would have assured her there was someone out there who'd care for her. With that assurance, she would not have settled for a bastard who convinced her he was her only shot at happiness.

Finally, the universe also needed to apologize for placing the bastard who was responsible for her lying in the hospital on the same planet as her.

Georgia swallowed the lump in her throat. Life was unfair. All Celeste ever wanted was to find someone to love her and father her children. Instead, she got someone who did not deserve an eighth of the happiness the woman had to give.

"They have to go now." Nonna Sophie laid a gentle hand on Georgia's arm.

She nodded before she leaned over her friend's

bed. She placed a kiss on Celeste's brow.

"I'll be here when you get out of surgery," she whispered.

She stepped back and allowed the older woman to wish her granddaughter well. They watched as the orderly and the nurse wheeled Celeste to the operating room to take care of the unborn child who had not survived the beating.

Georgia led the woman to the waiting room, where Mr. Santiano sat. He leaned forward with his elbows resting on his knees and his shoulders drooping.

"She's a strong girl." Nonna Sophie sat next to her son and hugged his shoulders. "She'll get through this."

"She's never hurt anyone," he said. "Why does she have to suffer?"

"We can never know why things happen the way they do. We can only accept that both good and bad things happen."

The older man shook his head. "I can't accept it."

"What happened?"

Georgia glanced toward the door. Dread filled Nicholas's eyes. She stood and walked over to him. Without a word, he followed her out of the room.

"Is she…"

Georgia shook her head. "No, they just wheeled her to surgery. Celeste was pregnant, and she lost the baby."

Nicholas tensed. "When she gets out, tell her she's a widow."

Georgia had no doubt Gianni was not among the living. After Mr. Santiano had saved the officer from Nicholas's rage, he'd made a few telephone calls. She knew he would want revenge for his daughter, but there was only so much blood he'd allow on his son's hands. The appropriate associates would have been dispatched to assure Gianni would never raise his hand to someone else again.

However, assuring Gianni no longer breathed was not good enough for her.

"Did he suffer?" she asked.

\*\*\*\*

Nicholas was certain he had not heard her correctly. Georgia was the most passive woman he knew. She never subscribed to the eye-for-an-eye belief.

The woman, however, did not blink. Lines marred her forehead as her eyes narrowed, her nose flared, and the corner of her lips turned down. She held her head high with her shoulders back, both hands balled tight.

"Did. He. Fucking. Suffer?" She hissed through clenched teeth.

She did not acknowledge the gasps from people who passed. The daggers in her eyes said she did not give a damn about the profanity she spewed. She wanted blood, and only the confirmation that much was spilled would pacify her.

"Yes, he did."

With a nod, Georgia turned and walked away. Though he needed her presence, Nicholas did not call out to her. There was too much shame in the role he'd played in his sister's predicament. Had he listened to Georgia, none of them would be there.

\*\*\*\*

Georgia stared at the tile floor outside her apartment. Though someone had mopped up the actual blood, she could still see the smear in her mind.

Nicholas slipped the key from her grip and unlocked the door. With a hand on her lower back, he led her into the apartment and closed the door behind them.

She dropped her handbag on the dresses that lay on the floor by the door and headed for the kitchen. She opened the cabinet under the sink and retrieved a bottle of moonshine her father had brought up the last time he visited the south. Though he had access to more quality liquor, he always said nothing had a kick like the homebrew he got from relatives.

Though Celeste had pulled through the surgery, the news they had received had not been good. The internal damage had been greater than the doctor at first believed. Her friend would never have children of her own.

Georgia had felt the chill when they were told. She had been so furious she'd wished Mr. Santiano had not ordered the elimination of his son-in-law. Gianni needed to suffer some more.

Georgia placed the bottle on the table and reached for two glasses from the dish dryer. She poured the equivalent of a shot in one glass and passed it to Nicholas. As he knocked back his drink, she poured herself a double.

She downed her drink. The liquid burned her throat and brought tears to her eyes. Yet it did not help her accomplish her goal. She could still feel. There was the pain over her friend's loss and the anger over Gianni's actions. She would not be content until she felt nothing.

Determined to achieve her goal, Georgia poured another shot. Before she could consume the liquor, Nicholas snatched the glass from her hand.

"You need to pace yourself. Do you know what this stuff will do to you?"

"Of course I do. Why the hell do you think I'm drinking it?" She reached for her drink. Nicholas held the glass out of her reach. "Give it back."

He shook his head.

Not in the mood to argue with him, she reached for the bottle. Nicholas set both glasses in the sink and snatched the bottle from her.

Georgia screeched, "Give it back!"

\*\*\*\*

Nicholas shook his head. "It won't solve anything."

Tears hovered at the brim of her eyes. "It'll make me forget."

He was not only tempted to oblige her but to pour the drinks himself. They could knock back one shot after another until neither one of them could remember the cruelty they'd witnessed. But eventually morning would come and they would have to deal with a hangover as well as reality.

Their other option was to turn to each other for comfort like they used to, before he became deaf, dumb, and blind to her concerns. Of course, there was a great chance she'd prefer the moonshine to his company.

Nicholas placed the bottle on the sink and extended a hand to her.

He held his breath as she stared at it. He did not know if she'd ever forgive him. Hell, he knew he'd never forgive himself.

After a heartbeat, Georgia stepped forward. Her arms encircled his waist, and her head rested on his chest. She held on tight, as if she got strength from him.

He wrapped his arms around her and relished the feel of her against him. For the moment, no one else mattered. It was just the two of them getting comfort from each other.

Nicholas kissed the top of her head, and she glanced up. Her eyes showed no reproach. Instead, he saw compassion. Her fingertips touched his cheek and, for the first time, he realized it was moist with tears. He covered her hand with his. She gently intertwined their fingers, then pulled his hand to her lips and kissed the bruised knuckles.

The kiss was as chaste as the ones he'd given her years ago when she scraped her knee jumping rope. Yet her touch created a spark that nearly knocked him to his knees.

****

On more than one occasion Georgia had watched Nicholas lust over a well-endowed woman in a tight sweater, sashaying down the street. Then there were the leers that broadcast every lewd thought running through his mind. Yet the heated glance he focused on her was more intense than any she had ever witnessed.

He dipped his head lower. Anticipating the kiss, she held her breath, but instead of covering her lips with his, he hesitated.

She knew the moment their lips touched there would be no turning back, and she suspected it was the biggest dilemma Nicholas had ever faced. Though he wanted her, she was supposed to be off limits to everyone but her husband.

When Nonna Sophie explained to Celeste and Georgia what went on between a man and woman in bed, she also stressed the act was supposed to be performed only after they got married. Only easy women, like the ones Nicholas dated, slept with a man before standing in front of a man of the cloth.

At that moment, Georgia did not give a damn about what good girls did and did not do. For just one night, she wanted to forget about virtues and simply do whatever it took to forget her pain.

Georgia reached up and swiped her tongue over his bottom lip. Beyond that move, she did not know what else to do. Nonna Sophie may have told them what happened in bed; she had omitted the instruction on how to get men there.

The tail on the cat clock hanging next to the refrigerator ticked off the time. With each passing second, her hope faded. He was going to be honorable; the type of man she should settle down with...not the type she needed at that moment.

Just as Georgia was prepared to walk away, Nicholas leaned in and pressed his lips to hers. Her body's reaction was as powerful as with their previous kiss. Her heart pounded against her chest, her breasts grew sensitive, and the throbbing between her legs returned.

Nicholas released her hand and palmed her breast. She trembled under his touch. If he could affect her despite the barrier of her shirt and bra, she wondered what he could achieve when her clothes were off.

His free hand gripped her wrist and directed her hand until she felt the object he had gone out of his way to hide from her for years. She hesitantly touched the firm body part, then ran her hand down the length and back up again. After performing that gesture two more times, she measured the diameter as best she could through his clothes.

Georgia slowly shook her head. A self-examination in the shower as a teenager had told her no part of her could accommodate that. He would tear her apart.

Nicholas broke the kiss. "Do you want to stop?"

She shook her head. "No, but you...how..." She paused. She could not voice her concern. It would remind him of her innocence.

"How will it fit?" he guessed.

Georgia felt her heart drop. She braced herself for his rejection. Surely he would not want to be with someone with so little experience, not when he had a bevy of women who knew their way around a bed.

**\*\*\*\***

Her question should have convinced him to leave. Georgia had so much going for her, she didn't need him complicating things. But, as he had done all his life...with school...with the club...with his career...he followed his wishes.

Nicholas took her hand and led her to the bedroom. He stopped on the threshold and surveyed the small space furnished with secondhand pieces obtained from Celeste when the latter redecorated her bedroom four years earlier. He barely glimpsed the oak dresser or the nightstand before he focused on the daybed across the room.

Georgia released Nicholas's hand and slipped her flats into the empty spot between her sandals and the short-heeled shoes that were lined next to the door. Following her example, he kicked off his shoes and placed them next to her dress heels.

When he turned back to her, Georgia had opened the first two buttons on her shirt and was fiddling with the third.

"Stop."

Georgia's hands dropped to her side. Her eyes begged him not to change his mind and walk out.

Had she been one of his other women, he would have welcomed her initiative, as it would have gotten them to their goal a lot quicker. However, he did not want to hurry up and find relief. He needed their time together to last.

Shaking his head, he stepped forward. "I want the pleasure," he whispered as he reached for the button she'd abandoned.

He slowly opened each button, kissing the exposed skin as he peeled away the material. Georgia shivered under his touch. Her groans confirmed her excitement.

Encouraged by her body's reaction, he slowly removed her clothes, dropping them on the floor until she was surrounded by a sea of material. He then gripped her wrists and held her arms from her sides. He could not let her cover herself until he committed every curve to memory. Their time together was probably a one-time deal, and he was determined to remember every detail, down to the inch-long, pear-shaped birthmark on her left thigh.

Nicholas stared until Georgia's gaze dropped to her feet. Respecting the courage it took for her to be with him, he led her to the bed. He pulled back the apple-green spread, then waited as she scrambled underneath the cover.

Georgia watched as Nicholas pulled the T-shirt over his head and tossed it on top of her clothes. Her eyes grew wide when he reached for his belt. She did not blink as he opened his pants and pushed them down his legs. Once they were far enough, he stepped out of them. Then he lifted each foot to pull off his socks.

He stood and waited as Georgia's gaze slowly moved up from his feet, taking in everything uncovered. When she reached his eyes, he held her gaze for a heartbeat before peeling off his boxer briefs. He bent to push them to the floor.

"Do you want to stop?" he asked as he stood up.

Georgia shook her head.

"Then look at me."

She cracked opened one eye and peeked at him. He remained still until she got the courage to open the other eye. Her mouth dropped open in an O. Her reaction would have flattered him had it not been a result of her inexperience. It did, however, serve as a reminder that he needed to move slow for her.

Nicholas picked up his pants, retrieved the only barrier that would come between them, and tossed one on the nightstand. He then crawled under the spread and lay on his side.

Knowing Georgia was comfortable kissing him; he leaned in and pressed his lips to hers. He suspected she would not respond to others as eagerly as she did with him. As always, she trusted and, this time, he refused to let her down.

When he finally moved his lips to her jawline, Georgia was on top. He chose the position to make her feel more in control of the situation. However, her hesitation indicated she felt self-conscious being on top and did not know what to do.

Nicholas maneuvered her legs until she straddled his hips. He then pushed up, grinding his groin into her. Georgia gasped. She reached forward and gripped his shoulders, her nails digging into the skin.

A surge shot through him. He had not considered the effect the move would have on his body. His body trembled, threatening to shatter.

Stars danced in front of his eyes, yet they did not entirely obscure his vision. He saw the bliss on Georgia's face and was determined to witness her orgasm.

Nicholas began to count backwards from one hundred. With his hands on her hips, he slowly slid her up and down his groin as he pushed into her. He continued until she found the rhythm. He then relaxed his grip and allowed her to move on her own.

Her legs clenched his sides as if she was afraid he would slip away. It was a fear she did not have to worry about. He was not going anywhere anytime soon. Of course, if he had his way, he would never leave her.

Georgia closed her eyes, and soft groans escaped from the back of her throat. The look of bliss on her face would forever be etched in Nicholas's mind. Despite all the women he had been with, he had never witnessed anything as beautiful Georgia's orgasm.

By the time she relaxed, he had rolled on a condom and shifted until she was on the bed and he was tucked between her thighs. He slowly slipped a finger into her. She stiffened, and her walls clenched on the digit. He pumped the finger in and out until she was relaxed enough for him to slip a second finger inside, into her moisture.

Knowing she was as ready as she would get, Nicholas withdrew his hand. He took a deep breath and positioned himself at her entrance.

Georgia tensed as his head pushed into her. He

stopped, allowing her to get adjusted to him and willing his body not to react to the tightness surrounding him. It was the most difficult task he'd ever performed, as he had been ready since she first kissed him.

The lines on Georgia's brow slowly disappeared. When she no longer appeared to be in discomfort, he pulled back, then pushed forward. Each withdrawal and reentry moved him farther into her, until he felt the barrier that had yet to be broken.

Nicholas stopped and stared at her. He needed to be sure it was something she wanted to do. Once he moved forward there would be no turning back.

Georgia reached up and brushed a finger over his jaw. "Go ahead."

Closing his eyes, Nicholas pulled back and then plunged in. Georgia tensed beneath him. He felt no joy in the deflowering. He had caused her pain instead of happiness, and he felt like a jerk for the role he played.

He remained still until he felt fingertips brush his cheek. He opened his eyes and stared at Georgia. Her tender look told him she didn't blame him for anything.

She nodded her head, and he began moving again. The length of time he had been trying to hold out and her tightness caused him to shudder after a minute, and he came without her.

Once there was nothing left in him, Nicholas pulled out and climbed off the bed. He removed the condom, secured the end, and dropped it in the trash bin by the desk near the window.

He returned to the bed and crawled back underneath the spread.

"How do you feel?" he asked.

Georgia lay back and shrugged her shoulders.

"I'm sorry I couldn't make it better for you." He looked away. "Damn, you must hate me."

\*\*\*\*

Georgia leaned up on one arm. She took his chin in her hand and turned his face to her. She shook her head; she could never hate him.

He had given her what she needed…a distraction from the harsh reality of life. For that, she would always be grateful to him.

Chapter 18

Nicholas knew he overstepped his bounds. Just because she offered him her body for one night, it didn't give him the right to take over her kitchen. However, after watching her beat an egg with bits of shell in the bowl, he had to nudge her aside with his hip, while he poured the concoction down the drain.

As hard as her father worked to make the money for the groceries, one would think she would take better care when preparing a meal.

"You can either stand there giving me the evil eye or you can enjoy your meal," he said, pointing to the plate in front of the empty chair.

With a huff, Georgia dropped into the chair across from him. Her glare said she would eat the food, but she'd be damned if she would compliment him. However, she could not suppress her moan of appreciation once a piece of omelet was in her mouth.

Instead of fishing for more compliments, Nicholas announced, "I'll wash the dishes while you take care of the bar."

She shook her head. "How am I ever going to repay you for everything?"

Nicholas shoveled a slice of bacon into his mouth to keep from blurting out suggestions. Like an addict, he needed another fix—in his case, more time with her. The previous evening had not been enough and, something told him, neither would another twenty-four hours in bed with her.

As Nicholas swallowed, a fist slammed against the front door. He dropped his fork onto his plate and pushed back from the table. He held out his hand, signaling Georgia to remain in her chair. First he would find out who had the audacity to make such a racket. Then he would teach the person some manners.

"Georgia, open this damn door!" a voice on the other side shouted.

She sucked her teeth. "It's only William."

Before Nicholas could warn her back, she dashed out of the kitchen. He reached the living room as she flung open the door.

"Why are you out there making that racket?"

"Where the hell have you been?" The irate man pushed passed her into the apartment. He stopped short when he saw Nicholas. "What the hell is he doin' here?"

"I'm not appreciating the tone," Georgia said, stepping between the two men. "Though I don't have to explain myself, Nick is here because Celeste is in the hospital."

The other man wrinkled his brow.

Georgia reminded him, "Celeste, my best friend, his sister."

"Then why the hell is he here and not at the hospital with her?"

"Nick drove me home last night, after visiting hours were over."

Nicholas was unsure if she realized she had confirmed he stayed overnight. William glanced at the sofa, untouched for days.

"You and him? How could you whore yourself out to a white man?"

Georgia's back stiffened. "Nick, could you please excuse us?" Her low tone indicated she was about to give her visitor a piece of her mind.

"I'd prefer to stay." He had an uneasy feeling about the other man and did not like the idea of her being in the apartment alone with him.

Instead of agreeing with him as he'd hoped she would, Georgia spun around and crossed her arms over her chest. She might not realize it, but she had different postures for each of her moods. Her hands behind her back meant she was about to tease him, and hands on her hips meant she was exasperated with him. But arms crossed over her chest meant she was good and mad.

"Nicholas, leave."

The use of his full name and the absence of the word "please" had him stepping around her. He continued to the door.

"Close the door behind you," she ordered once he was in the hall.

He hesitated. Instead of repeating herself, she marched over and pushed the door closed in his face. Realizing he would not hear a thing unless she started to yell, Nicholas continued down the stairs. He reasoned it was best he was not around when the other man left. He might give in to the temptation to relocate the man's teeth to another state.

\*\*\*\*

"The minute your father's out of the picture, you turn into a whore."

Georgia walked back into the living room. She felt bad for kicking Nicholas out of the apartment, but she did not want him to get into a fight with William. His presence would only fuel the other man's anger, and she was not in the mood to clean up the destruction caused by two men trying to prove who was more macho.

Besides, what did he expect after they spent the night together? People did not usually look favorably at women who slept with men out of wedlock.

Though she was willing to accept that others might not think highly of her, she did not have to accept them talking down to her.

"I don't appreciate your tone."

"And I don't appreciate you runnin' all over town with him. You need to remember who you are."

"Is your problem that I'm with another man, or that I'm with a white man?"

William sucked his teeth.

She crossed her arms over her chest and tapped her foot. "Well, what is it?"

"It don't matter. You need to stay away from him."

"It does matter."

"Why?"

"Because I need to know how tolerant you are." She pointed to the picture on the wall. "Remember, my mother was Filipino."

"That's different."

"How so?"

"'Cause I said so."

"That's not good enough. How about another question? How do you feel about Celeste?"

William snorted. "I don't have to answer to you."

"That was answer enough for me." Georgia walked to the door and opened it. "You need to leave."

William chuckled. He walked toward her and shoved the door out of her grip.

"I'll go when I'm damn well good and ready."

"Screw you."

Georgia did not register the hand swinging toward her until it was too late to move. The side of her face stung, and she momentarily saw bright lights.

"It's about time you remember your place. I'm not going to take any more of your lip. Now go clean yourself up."

She waited until her vision cleared before she stepped around him. She slowly made her way down the hall. As she stepped into her bedroom, he called out, "Screw me? You up here screwin' everyone else, the least you could do is screw me."

****

"Are you some kind of idiot, or what?"

"It's nice seeing you too, Pops," Nicholas greeted, though he did not glance up from the bar he was wiping. "We ain't open for business, but I'm sure Georgia wouldn't mind if you had a drink." He waved at the mostly empty shelf behind him. "Pick your poison."

"You're lucky I'm not picking you off the floor."

"Sounds like you're a bit displeased with me." Nicholas glanced up. "You care to share why?"

"I stopped by your place earlier, and you weren't there."

"Yeah, kind of hard for me to be in two places at once."

"I asked you to drop Georgia off last night. Tell me you didn't stay."

"Can't tell you a lie."

"Then tell me you slept in separate rooms."

Nicholas made no sound.

His father slammed his fist on the bar. "You slept with her," he shouted.

"And what's wrong with Georgia?"

"She's not like those bimbos you keep company with. Georgia's a good girl. She shouldn't be mixed up with a thug like you."

Nicholas threw the washrag across the room. "You don't think I know that?" He leaned against the wall and gripped his head.

"Then why?"

"Because I couldn't walk away from her. Trust me, I've tried, but the more I argue the reasons why I shouldn't be with her, the more I want her."

His father stared at him a second, before he seemed to deflate. His shoulders drooped as he sank onto a stool, rested his elbows on the bar, and dropped his head in his hands.

"They have a way of doing that."

"What?" Nicholas dropped his hands to his side.

His father lifted his head. "Your mother had the same effect on me." He wiped his hand over his face.

Figuring the conversation would not be an easy one for the older man, Nicholas grabbed a bottle of scotch. He retrieved two glasses from under the bar and poured each of them a drink.

His father stared at his glass but made no attempt to take it.

"I first saw your mother at a cousin's wedding. She was the maid of honor, and I can honestly say, to this day, I don't know what the bride wore. From the moment your mother came down the aisle, I could not take my eyes off her. I spent the day staring at her and the next two weeks thinking about her. When the bride and groom returned from their honeymoon, I questioned my cousin's wife until she offered to have a dinner party and invite us over.

"When I was finally introduced to your mother, I knew she was not the type of woman I could bed a few times and then walk away from. I had to have her forever." His father looked up and shook a finger at him. "However, even though I realized that, I did not lay a hand on her until we were married."

"Okay, so maybe last night was not the smartest thing I've ever done," Nicholas said. "However, I'm not sorry I did it."

"Then what are your intentions?"

Nicholas shook his head. "I'm not sure."

"Then let me give you a piece of advice." His father did not wait to see if his advice was wanted or not. "I didn't do entirely right by your mother."

"Whaddaya mean? Did you cheat on her?"

"No, I was never unfaithful to your mother. And if you ever suggest it again, I'll deck you."

Nicholas nodded.

"I knew your mother was not thrilled with my career choice, but, nonetheless, I stayed with it. It was the one thing I did that made her unhappy. If I had to do it over again, I'd quit the business and do something legitimate. You already know Georgia doesn't approve of your lifestyle. Are you willing to give up your business to make her happy? If not, you need to back off."

It was one of the things Nicholas had considered as he held Georgia during the night. He enjoyed the excitement of a good hustle, yet it was not the lifestyle she should be involved with. She needed a good man who was willing to go out and make an honest living.

He raised his glass. Before it reached his lips, a pop echoed from overhead.

Nicholas slammed the glass on the bar and dashed to the back. His father followed him upstairs. With no thought about what was on the other side, he flung open the door and ran into the apartment. He stopped short in the foyer. A chill rushed through him.

Georgia stood at the entrance to the hall. She ignored the blood dripping from her nose. Her arms were stretched out in front of her. Both hands clutched a gun. William cowered on the floor behind the sofa.

As much as Nicholas wanted to go after the other man, Georgia was his first priority. He moved to her side slowly so as not to spook her.

"Georgia, honey, put the gun down."

She shook her head. "He was man enough to hit me; he should be man enough to face me."

"You can't shoot him."

"I'm no one's punching bag."

"I know you're not, darling."

"No one's going to hurt me like Celeste."

"I'm not going to let anyone hurt you." Nicholas placed a hand over hers. "Most of all, I'm not going to let you hurt yourself."

She glanced at him.

"I can't let you get blood on your hands. Please, give me the gun."

Georgia lowered her arms. Nicholas took the gun from her as his father stepped forward and grabbed William by his collar.

"I'll take care of him," his father announced.

Nicholas held out the gun. "Take this with you."

His father took the weapon, then dragged the other man to the front door of the apartment, where he shoved William through the neighbors who had gathered to watch the drama.

"Where'd you get the gun?" Nicholas asked once the door closed.

"Joey gave it to me."

Nicholas shook his head as he pulled her to him. Georgia was changing, and he could not allow that to happen. He hadn't protected Celeste, or Gracie's. He would be damned if he did not save Georgia from herself.

"You won't need that as long as I'm around," he whispered, hoping he had not been too late for her.

Chapter 19

"I'd like to know where you find your men, so I can avoid that place."

Neither Celeste nor Georgia smiled at the nurse's tasteless joke. After a few seconds of cold silence, the other woman realized the friends did not find humor in the bruises they sported. She quickly gathered the soiled bandages she had changed and exited the room.

"How are you feeling?" Georgia kissed her friend's forehead.

"Forget me." Celeste brushed the tender bruise under Georgia's right eye with an index finger. "What the hell happened to you?"

"William and I had a disagreement."

"William? Who's that?"

Georgia remembered Celeste had never met the man her father had such high hopes for. She quickly got her friend caught up with her life.

"You told your father?"

Georgia flinched as she recalled her father's reaction. She had stopped to go over the liquor order and give him an update on the furniture repairs. Since his injuries had not included a temporary loss of vision, he immediately noticed the bruise on her face.

Her father had been livid. He ranted for ten minutes, threatening to walk out in his pajamas to search for William. He finally calmed down when Mr.

Santiano arrived and assured her father that once William's hand healed, the man would think twice before raising it to another woman.

"I'm sorry you had to go through that," Celeste sympathized.

"You and me both." With a sigh, Georgia dropped into the chair. "I should be grateful he showed his true colors before we got serious."

"Were you thinking about marrying him?"

Georgia shook her head. The previous night she had made up her mind to tell William they could only be friends. He was nothing like Nicholas, and she could not settle for someone who had not made her feel as special as her friend did.

"At least you don't have to learn that happily-ever-after is a bunch of bull. All these happy couples in the movies...humph. I wish they would stop filling women's heads with dreams and show the reality of marriage."

"What are you talking about?"

Celeste slumped back. "The moment Gianni said, 'I do,' he changed. All he cared about was his wants and needs. Screw whatever I wanted."

Georgia cringed at her friend's language. The light had been extinguished from her eyes. She looked like her soul had been sucked from her, leaving a jaded shell.

"Not all men are like..."

Celeste's glare chilled Georgia. Her friend did not want to hear a line that not all men were jerks. And she did not want to be assured that there was someone decent out there for her.

Gianni had not only taken Celeste's innocence but

228

had conned the woman into a relationship by making her believe there was no one else out there who'd accept her. She no longer wore her rose-colored glasses, and for that change in her Georgia wished Nicholas could go another round with his brother-in-law.

"We walked out of the courthouse, and he couldn't wait till we got to the hotel to start our wedding night."

A dread filled Georgia.

"He had parked the car in an isolated area of the parking lot. When we returned to it, he ordered me to remove my underwear and climb into the back seat. When I insisted we wait, he grabbed me by the neck, waved the marriage certificate in my face, and told me that piece of paper gave him the right to be with me whenever and wherever he wanted."

"He made you do it in the car, against your will?"

Celeste took a ragged breath. "Nonna said the first couple of times might not be pleasant, but she never told us how awful it would be. It felt like he was ripping into me."

Georgia thought about Nicholas. It had felt weird with him inside her, filling her until she did not think she could stretch any more. And the tearing of her maidenhead did hurt, but even that pain had subsided.

"Did the sex get better?"

Celeste shook her head. "The only thing that made it all worthwhile was when the doctor told me I was pregnant." She placed her hand on her stomach. "I had gone to the doctor just before I visited your father."

"Why didn't you say anything?"

"I hadn't told Gianni yet. I had planned to surprise him over dinner, but when Nicholas insisted we eat at the club, I decided to put it off for another day."

"Did you ever get a chance to tell him?"

"When he got home that night, he was so mad I figured I'd tell him to make him happy." Celeste turned her head and stared past Georgia. "He accused me of sleeping around and said the baby wasn't his."

Georgia swallowed back the bile in her throat. She would not fall apart in Celeste's presence. Her friend needed her to be strong. She would save her breakdown for another time…when she was alone…or better yet, when she was with Nicholas, who would comfort her.

"I wish you would've told us."

"I thought if I did everything he asked, things would get better."

"I hope you don't believe any of this is your fault."

"Of course it is. I was stupid enough to believe in all that romance crap. That's a fantasy…at least for someone who looks like me."

By the time Georgia walked out of the room, it was as though someone had sucked all the energy from her.

"What's wrong?" Nicholas stood as Georgia stepped into the lounge. He had waited in the other room to give the women a chance to talk privately.

Georgia heard the fear in his voice and intended to ease his worries. But when she opened her mouth, the emotions she had forced back during her visit rushed to the surface. She stepped out of the room and dashed down the hall to the bathroom. She slammed into the room and headed to the nearest stall. Without bothering to close the door, she dropped to her knees and emptied her stomach into the toilet.

Once there was nothing left to bring up, she felt a hand on her back. She glanced up as another hand reached out and depressed the lever, sending away the remains of her breakfast.

With his hands on her waist, Nicholas pulled her to her feet and led her to the sink. The door opened as he turned on the faucet.

"It's occupied," he barked in response to the older woman's squeak. When she simply glared back at them, he released Georgia and marched to the door. "Find another bathroom," he ordered.

The woman backed up until she was on the other side of the threshold. Nicholas closed the door and shoved the trashcan under the doorknob.

"Maybe we should go," Georgia suggested.

He shook his head as he moved back to her side. He pointed to the water. "Drink."

With a sigh, Georgia cupped her hands under the faucet and filled them with the lukewarm water. She slurped up the liquid and sloshed it around in her mouth before spitting it into the sink. She would have preferred a toothbrush and toothpaste but figured the water would suffice for the time being.

Nicholas wetted a paper towel, then wiped her face, taking care around the bruise. Once he'd finished, he turned off the faucet and leaned against the sink.

"What happened?"

Georgia had no desire to revisit the conversation she'd had with Celeste. The determined look in Nicholas's eyes said he would get the information, even if he had to ask his sister.

Not wanting her friend to have to relive her nightmare for the second time in less than an hour, Georgia leaned against the wall.

"Gianni started beating on her the moment they walked out of the courthouse."

Other than an occasional flinch, Nicholas showed no outward sign of his emotions as she revealed the beatings his sister had endured. She did not discuss the coupling between them, as she felt the other woman deserved a bit of privacy.

"How could I have been so blind?"

Georgia stepped in front of Nicholas and wrapped her arms around his waist. "You'd known Gianni for years. You didn't want to think the worst of your friend."

**** 

Nicholas shook his head. There had been the signs. Besides her warning, he'd seen the changes not only in Celeste but in Gianni. The other man's behavior had been more abrupt, and he'd demonstrated the physical signs of a user.

"I'm not going to let you blame yourself for this," Georgia mumbled in his chest.

"Why shouldn't you?"

She lifted her head. Her eyes narrowed. "I just finished listening to Celeste blame herself for not being the ideal wife. Now you're kicking yourself for not listening to me or seeing the signs. However, no one has said a thing against Gianni. He's the one who lifted a hand to Celeste." She took a deep breath and slowly exhaled. "If anything, Celeste needs to be commended for leaving before he killed her. As for you…" She intertwined her fingers through his, lifted his hand to her lips, and kissed his battered knuckles.

Nicholas did not deserve Georgia's comfort. She was a good woman and deserved better than him. Yet he vowed that as long as she was turning to him she was never going to regret giving him a second chance.

He flinched at the rattle of the doorknob. A second later, someone pounded on the door.

"What's going on in there?" a deeper voice asked.

Nicholas opened his mouth to reply. A hand covered his mouth, preventing him from cursing the intruder.

"This is the ladies' room," Georgia reminded him. She stepped back and tugged on his hand. "Come on."

He reluctantly pushed away from the sink and followed her to the door. She rolled her eyes when he kicked the trashcan to the side. He showed no remorse as he snatched open the door and glared at the woman he had forced out of the bathroom and the nurse and two orderlies who now accompanied her.

"What were you doing in there?" the nurse asked.

"Minding my own damn business," Nicholas replied. "You should try it one day."

Ignoring the woman's gasp, he marched down the hall.

"Nick, that was rude," Georgia scolded.

He stopped in front of the elevator and pressed the call button.

When he did not reply, she asked, "Don't you have anything to say?"

"You feel like going for a ride?"

Georgia threw up her free hand and huffed, but she didn't argue when they climbed into his car and he headed in the direction opposite of her apartment.

****

Georgia dropped back onto Nicholas's bed and sighed. The drive to Coney Island and a walk along the boardwalk had done little to lighten their moods. She became more depressed when they stopped in the diner and caught a glimpse of the black eye Mr. Santiano had given Joey for supplying her with a gun.

It felt like the fates were determined to make their lives as miserable as possible. As soon as she found a way to cope with one trial, another tribulation reared its head.

A soft rap on the door was followed by, "May I come in?"

"Yes," she replied as she sat up.

Nicholas cracked open the door and stuck his head into the room. "I wanted to get my things before you went to bed."

Georgia smiled. He did not assume they were sharing the bed, despite the previous evening's activities.

"I don't want you sleeping on sofa."

"I'm not gonna let you sleep on it."

"We could share the bed." Georgia was unaware of where she found the courage to make the suggestion and go after him to take his hand.

Feeling more confident than she had the previous evening, Georgia reached up and pressed her lips to his. There was no doubt in her mind that she wanted another night with him. She would take as many as he was willing to give her, as long as each time they were together he made her forget there was anyone else in the world.

Nicholas's kiss was more intense than their previous ones. She felt more of an urgency and longing behind it. Knowing how much he desired her made her want him more.

Georgia pulled his shirt from his pants and slipped her hand underneath. He shivered under her touch but did not pull back.

As she fingered the hairs covering his chest, he reached between them and unbuttoned her blouse. He pushed aside the fabric and caressed her breast through her bra.

His attention proved he was nothing like Celeste's husband. His first priority was not his needs, which gave her hope that each time she was with him, things could only get better.

Georgia pushed his shirt higher, until he broke off the kiss and pulled it off. They quickly shed their clothes, and Georgia crawled onto the bed.

Nicholas tossed his wallet onto the nightstand, then straddled her body. He leaned in and teased her breasts with his tongue. Tapping into the part of her that allowed her to take chances, she reached down and touched him, marveling at his smoothness. He was firm and, despite what he insisted, she still believed he was rather big.

As she encircled him with her hand, Nicholas reached between them and guided her to move from his base to his tip. He wore a look of concentration on his face, and when she did as he indicated, he hissed. Nicholas pulled back from her as he reached for his wallet and got out a condom. Once he was fully sheathed, he settled between her legs.

Nicholas hooked an arm under her right leg and bent it back, then slowly pushed inside her. It was a tight fit, yet there was no pain. Once he entered as far as he could go, he stopped and allowed her to adjust to him.

This time, she enjoyed his fullness. She felt her muscles contract.

"No, don't," Nicholas moaned. "I want it to last."

Understanding the effect she had on him, Georgia relaxed. She waited three seconds before she contracted her muscles again. At the same time, she raised her pelvis.

"Don't." Nicholas shook his head. "You're killing me."

Georgia relaxed again, before she did the same thing one more time. The third time was the charm. Nicholas withdrew until only his tip remained in her. He then plunged back in, eliciting a gasp from her. He continued to move, taking care to grind his groin against hers with each entry.

The movement caused the pressure to build once again. Eager to find relief, she met him thrust for thrust until, with one final push, their bodies shook and she saw lights before her eyes.

After what seemed like hours but was probably less than a minute, Nicholas lowered his body onto hers. He was hot and sweaty, yet Georgia relished the closeness of his body as he wrapped his arms around her.

\*\*\*\*

Nicholas felt a sense of loss. He opened his eyes and, in the moonlight, he found the answer.

Sometime during the night, Georgia had rolled away from him. The need for contact was new to him. His entire life he had been content to have his space in bed. But now, for the first time, he longed to hold someone.

As he considered the arrangement, he realized it was not just anyone he wanted. It was Georgia. The only woman he had ever shared his bed with.

Nicholas reached across the empty space and

considered trading in the queen-sized bed for a twin. At least she wouldn't have far to go when she rolled away from him.

"What's wrong?" Georgia mumbled as she rolled back to him.

"I wanted to hold you," he whispered.

She snuggled against him. "Anytime you want."

Nicholas leaned forward and kissed the top of her head. He hoped she meant it, because he planned to hold her to her word.

Chapter 20

"Do you have to smoke that thing over there?" Mr. Collins grumbled.

Nicholas glanced at the cigarette he had lit. "No, I could bring it closer to you."

"Always got to be a wiseass."

Nicholas crushed the cigarette in the ashtray, then moved from the windowsill to the chair. What was one day, he figured. If Georgia's father lived to be a hundred, he'd have a little over fifty more years to aggravate the man. He would therefore have plenty of other opportunities to amuse himself.

"Isn't there a nurse you have to chase?"

"My skirt-chasing days are over."

"Since when?"

"Since I'm marrying your daughter."

His future father-in-law raised an eyebrow. "Aren't you supposed to ask my permission?"

"I would if I thought there was a chance in hell you'd give it to me."

"And Georgia actually agreed to marry you without my consent?"

"I haven't told her yet."

"You haven't told her?" Mr. Collins alternated between chuckling and groaning from the pain caused by the laughter. "Do me a favor and wait till I'm there before you tell her."

"You don't think she'll agree?" Nicholas asked, assuming the other man wanted to witness the rejection.

"No, she'll marry you, after she gives you what for. Even as a child that girl never liked being told what to do." After a minute, the man sobered. "I hope you are not askin' her 'cause you have to?"

"No, sir." Nicholas had made sure he wore a condom each time they were together. But, unlike in his other relationships, he had not worn the protection to ensure he remained childless but to protect her from the stigma of becoming an unwed mother.

"But it's safe to assume she won't be a blushing bride."

Nicholas realized an honest answer to the question was potentially more dangerous than a lie. If the other man took exception to his daughter's lack of innocence, he could complain to Nicholas's father, who would have no problem sending someone to deal with the offense. Nevertheless, he refused to start building a relationship with his future father-in-law on a lie.

"No, sir. She won't."

Mr. Collins took a deep breath and shook his head. "All I ever wanted was for her to have things easier than me and be happy. I sent her to college so she could find a husband, not so she could work in a diner."

"Excuse me?"

"The two of you seriously thought I didn't know about the job? As soon as Joey made the offer, your father called me. I knew she wasn't going to turn down that opportunity."

"Why didn't you want her to work?"

"'Cause she was my princess, and princesses shouldn't work. They should be treated like royalty, and cared for."

"I plan to provide for her...legitimately. I'm getting out of the numbers game."

The other man snorted.

"I figured you'd be happy with the news. I know you never approved of how I earned my money."

"That never mattered to me. If people want to throw their money away, that's their business."

"If it wasn't that, then why don't you like me?"

"'Cause you're white, boy."

Nicholas jerked at the admission. He'd never suspected the other man was prejudiced, especially since his wife was Filipino.

"Georgia was five when I turned my back on her at the grocery store. Some old witch came up to her and read her palm. She said she saw blue eyes in my baby's future. I ran that witch off and told Georgia never to let anyone do readin's on her or get her involved with roots. I then forgot about the incident until I met you. From the moment I met you, I knew that witch was talking about you and you'd be a part of my baby's life forever."

"Don't you think it's kind of hypocritical of you, considering Georgia's mother?"

"No, 'cause I'm comin' at you as a father who doesn't want to see his daughter hurt. Y'all get together, and there'll be plenty of people who'll wanna do y'all harm. Georgia told me about the fights you got into 'cause some idiot called her out of her name. Take it from me: marryin' her won't make things easier. Her mother was disowned when she married me. Things were only marginally better when we went down south, with half my family wishin' me well and the other half callin' me a traitor to my own people."

"So you're saying, sir, that if you knew back then what you know now, you'd never marry Georgia's mother?" It seemed kind of odd, considering the picture of Georgia's mother that hung in her living room.

"The only person I've ever loved as much as Georgia was her mother. But honestly, if I'd known, I'm not sure if I'd ever have subjected her to what she had to go through. Bein' disowned from her family and shunned by her in-laws—she had it rough."

Nicholas was grateful for the warning from the other man. However, he could not walk away from Georgia unless she said she wanted nothing to do with him. As any addict would be, he was being selfish and putting the decision in her lap.

With a nod, Nicholas stood. "Thank you, sir, for your honesty."

"You're still gonna ask her?"

"Yes, sir. I wanna wake up next to Georgia every morning, and I'm willing to fight anyone who has something to say about it."

Mr. Collins nodded his head, a glint of respect in his eyes.

Nicholas walked around the bed, on his way out. He stopped at the door and turned back to the older man.

"Out of curiosity, sir, do you know whether your wife would have done things differently?"

The older man shook his head and chuckled. "If I had left the choice up to her, she'd have told me to stop bein' a fool and get my ass to the altar."

****

"What are we doing here?" Georgia asked as they

wandered into Gracie's

"I wanted to look around," Nicholas replied, surveying the dining room.

With no one else in the venue, he was able to remember what the place used to look like when his father ran things. Men wearing their best suits and women dressed to impress had frequented the establishment. The floors had been clean and the tables covered with fine linen. The food and entertainment had earned them many glowing reviews in the newspapers.

"What do you plan to do with the place?"

He shrugged. "I may invest in it."

"If you do, could you do me one favor?"

"What's that?"

"Hire a decent chef." She scrunched her face in disgust. "Bologna sandwiches do not belong on a menu."

Nicholas agreed. However, before he made any decisions, he needed someone to look at the books, and the only person he trusted with the job was standing beside him.

He led her to the back office. The last time he'd been there, he thought she had turned her back on them. Though he could not bring himself to ask her the details, from the recent events he was certain Gianni was responsible for her missing Celeste's party. And he also knew he would spend the rest of his life trying to make things right for that slight.

Georgia sat down as he searched through the desk until he found the ledger in the center drawer.

"Would you mind looking over the books?" He perched on the edge of the desk. "Of course, there's probably another set of books in here somewhere. If I find them, do you think you'll be able to make heads or tails of them?"

"I can try."

He saw the hope in her eye and was certain she could read his mind. However, he would not voice his thoughts until she confirmed whether there was a chance of fixing the mess his former brother-in-law had created. If the business was beyond saving, he would ask her to help him search for something they could do together during the day, before they retired together in the evening.

For some, that was too much time to spend together. But he figured the day he got tired of being with her was the day they needed to commit him.

Nicholas leaned forward and gave in to the urge to kiss her. Jimmie Rodgers's woman may have "Kisses Sweeter Than Wine," but hers were not as addictive as Georgia's.

Before the kiss got too intense and one thing led to another, a knock on the door forced them apart.

"I hope I'm interrupting something," his father announced, opening the door.

"Oh, my God," Georgia mumbled as she covered her face with her hand.

Nicholas stood up and glared at his father. The man could have let them finish, or at least spared Georgia the embarrassment of getting caught.

"You're following me?"

"I had a talk with James." His father sat on the sofa. "Are you serious?"

Though he realized the older man was not talking about the business, he decided to give his assessment of the club. "It's not a total loss. It'll take some hard work, but I think we can get the business back to what it was."

His father nodded. "I'll take your word for it."

"Did you speak to Celeste?"

"She doesn't want anything to do with the club. I figured I'd clean it up and sell it for her."

"How much are you asking?"

His father cocked an eyebrow. "You interested in buying it?"

"I was thinking it's time to retire from my current line of business."

"What…" Georgia stared at him.

He nodded.

"If you're serious, Alton could help you," his father suggested.

"I thought he quit." Considering everything that had happened over the past couple of days, Nicholas suspected otherwise.

"No, he didn't. I went to see him yesterday. He said Gianni started selling out the club the moment he took over. When Alton protested, he was taken out back and made an example of."

"What did they do?" Georgia asked.

"A broken leg and three cracked ribs."

"Jesus."

The number of casualties of Gianni's viciousness continued to grow. Nicholas wondered how many people the man had affected…how many could have been spared if he had listened to Georgia.

She slipped her hand in his. As always, he found comfort in her simple touch.

"Why didn't he come to you?" she asked.

"They threatened to go after his family next," his

father replied. "He felt it was best to keep quiet and move on. With Gianni gone, he can return to help you."

"Tell him he's welcome back, and he'll be compensated for his injuries," Nicholas said.

"I already took care of that. The only problem I see is your cook. He left with Alton and has already found another job."

"I'm not worried." He was certain he'd be able to convince a few family members to roll up their sleeves and help until he felt comfortable managing the kitchen on his own.

His father stood up and reached into his jacket pocket. He pulled out a small box and handed it to Nicholas.

He leaned over and kissed Georgia's temple. "You're a good girl, *cara*." He then patted Nicholas on the shoulder before he walked out of the room.

\*\*\*\*

"What were you talking about?" Georgia asked. "I only understood half the conversation."

If the men had meant for the conversation to be a secret, they would have asked her to give them a few minutes and waited until she left the room before continuing.

"I had a talk with your father today."

That did not sound promising. Nicholas went out of his way to aggravate her father, while the older man contemplated various ways he could keep the younger one away from her.

Reluctantly she asked, "What about?"

"I told him you're marrying me."

Georgia's mouth dropped open. He couldn't be serious. Not the Nicholas Santiano who once said he'd

Ursula Renée

take a vow of celibacy before he took a vow of marriage.

"I'm serious." He opened the box his father had handed to him. A white-gold diamond ring with leaves on either side rested in velvet. It was the same ring his mother wore in her wedding pictures.

"But what about—"

"My business? As I just told Pops, I'm ready to retire. Find something with a bit more stability. Like working in a kitchen."

"Then there's—"

"Your career. I figured you'd be able to juggle working at both the diner and the club."

"But I'm not—"

"No, you're definitely not like the women I used to go out with. That's why I'm proposing to you, not them."

She folded her arms over her chest and slumped in the chair.

"You have any more questions?"

"I'm sure if I did, you'd answer them before I finished getting the words out."

Nicholas cocked an eyebrow.

"Does that mean you're going to actually let me ask one?"

"Of course. I just did."

Georgia dropped her head back with a huff. Nicholas chuckled as he took her left hand. The smooth metal band slipped onto her finger.

She lifted her head and smiled. Nicholas was down on one knee in front of her.

"What about my father?"

"He doesn't like me, and he thinks you could do

246

better."

"And?"

"I personally don't think you'll ever find someone like me."

Georgia laughed. "Seriously."

"He'd also prefer you to marry a colored man and make life easier for both of us."

She dropped her head.

"But he'll always be in our corner." Nicholas hooked a finger under her chin and nudged her until she raised her head. "Georgia Mae Collins, will you marry me?"

Georgia never expected Nicholas would utter those four words without a gun pointed at his head or a well-endowed woman with a swollen belly standing in front of him.

At times, he could get too full of himself and needed to be taken down a peg. And, though he was abandoning his illegal activities, she was certain it was the only change he was making. He would never be able to walk away from someone who had a problem calling her by name. Instead, he would let his fists express his displeasure.

However, he had always been in her corner, cheering her on and supporting her dreams. And, though there were times they had their disagreements, he was always there for her when she needed him the most.

Though Georgia was certain her father would want her to consider the difficulties she would face being with Nicholas, she did not need to think about it. Nicholas was right—she'd never find a friend like him.

## A word about the author…

Ursula Renée wrote short stories in high school and poetry in college. She began writing novels while recuperating from arthroscopic surgery. When she is not writing, she enjoys drawing, photography, and stone carving.

Visit Ursula at:

www.ursularenee.com
blog.ursularenee.com